A Fine and Private Place

Also available in the Laurentian Library:

Morley Callaghan's Stories
The Loved and the Lost
The Many Colored Coat
Strange Fugitive
That Summer in Paris
A Passion in Rome

Morley Callaghan

A FINE AND PRIVATE PLACE

MACMILLAN OF CANADA
A Division of Gage Publishing Limited
Toronto, Canada

Originally published in hardcover in 1975 by
The Macmillan Company of Canada under
ISBN 0-7705-1277-1.

First Laurentian Library edition, 1983.

CANADIAN CATALOGUING IN PUBLICATION DATA
  Callaghan, Morley, 1903-
    A fine and private place

  (Laurentian library ; 80)
  ISBN 0-7715-9861-0

  I. Title. II. Series.

  PS8505.A41F5 1983   C813'.52   C83-098749-5
  PR9199.3.C343F5 1983

Cover design by Brant Cowie/Artplus

Macmillan of Canada
A Division of Gage Publishing Limited

Printed in Canada

Eugene Shore and his wife lived in a big house near the foot-bridge over a ravine. The ravine protected the Shores' affluent neighborhood from the swarming apartment life and busy subway entrance on the other side. At nighttime the hundreds of lighted apartment windows were like a golden screen keeping poorer people behind the screen away from the Shores' side of the ravine. Their house, with its shuttered windows, was covered with wisteria, and in June the vines were heavy with mauve blossoms that hung like bunches of grapes.

Every afternoon that winter on his walk downtown, even when it was snowing, Shore crossed the bridge in his beaver coat and beaver hat, wearing a suit that looked as if he had put it on that morning and had now forgotten what he was wearing. He didn't have to care, anyway. Little tufts of gray hair curled out from under his hat at the ears. He had such a solid fresh-faced air of well-being as he loafed along that no one would have believed he was a man who delighted in criminals and sometimes got them mixed up with saints. No one had ever looked at him that closely and wondered what he was up to.

Although Shore had been there all his life, always coming back no matter where he went in the world, no one knew how

1

he earned his living. On one occasion his next door neighbor, J.J. Coulson, an investment banker who at the time was at home nursing a bad case of hemorrhoids and was out watering his lawn, saw Shore passing. He called out to him.

"Hello, neighbor. You been out in the suburbs recently? Astonishing, the way it's grown out to the west." He'd been visiting there the other night, Coulson said. His son had bought a place.

Shore, after reflecting, said, "Hmm! I never go out to the suburbs. What does go on out there?" He made Coulson feel that he would be slumming if he went into the suburbs.

His back now up a little, Coulson remembered that he had seen some strange, scruffy-looking characters getting out of taxis late at night and going into the Shores' place. He thought they must have some dubious connections, so he said: "You know, neighbor, I've lived next door to you for more than ten years and I'm still not sure what you do for a living."

"Really?" Shore said blandly. "I put rice bowls outside my front door. Haven't you noticed people filling them?" And he went on his way.

Loafing around downtown he was always meeting someone who knew him. Lawyers he encountered wondered why he didn't practice law. He would have done well, they said. By now he might have been a judge. He looked like a judge with his self-assured, authoritative air. And he was known by some of the fight fans. Old Sam Ivey, a fight promoter, used to telephone Shore and have him come and sit in his box. He was flattered when Mrs. Shore sometimes came. Also downtown was Shore's only intellectual friend, a Hungarian furrier named H. Kadar who had once repaired Shore's beaver coat. When Shore came into the little fur shop for a visit on a Wednesday afternoon, the furrier's eyes would light up. He would take Shore into the cutting room, and over many cups of coffee they would talk about the great days of the theater in Vienna before World War II.

Not all of Shore's closer acquaintances lived outside his neighborhood. Sam Hennessey, who lived two blocks away,

2

was his friend. Hennessey, a burly mining engineer who built dams on rivers north of Lake Superior, liked women, and traveling in the Orient, and being rude to his neighbors. Every Thursday evening, after Shore had played poker at the Hennessey house, neighbors who liked to look out their windows late at night would see him coming slowly along the street, a little drunk, but maintaining his aplomb beautifully. But they didn't hold the coarse Hennessey against Shore; he was so polite and friendly when you met him on the street.

The street was the only place they did meet him. Even so, at such times he seemed to talk their language, and he didn't dress like a Gypsy. He was a good neighbor. What was a good neighbor? Well, a good neighbor was someone who kept his grass cut in the summer, his leaves raked in the fall, and the sidewalk in front of his house clear of ice in the winter.

Mrs. Shore, who was a sweet woman, was quiet. However, charming as she was, she was blamed for a little habit that rankled. The Shores, while accepting invitations to dinner, never asked anyone to their house. No one could say what went on in the big house. No one could say why the Shores preferred to go to Rome, Paris, or Mexico City in the winter rather than Barbados or the Bahamas like everyone else.

One of the Shores' neighbors, Mrs. Watson, an elegant woman whose industrialist husband was a heavy contributor to the Civic Ballet, was crossing the footbridge one winter day when she saw Mr. Shore coming toward her. It was windy, cold, and snowing, and she had on her mink coat and Spanish-leather highboots. She was walking her golden Labrador retriever. Mr. Shore was wearing his beaver coat and beaver hat.

"How do you do, Mr. Shore? I was hoping I would run into you." The wind, sweeping the snow down the ravine against them, made it difficult for them to look directly at each other. Their faces were red from the cold. The big dog jumped up at Mr. Shore who rubbed it under the chin.

"A funny thing happened to me," she said. "We were driving back from Acapulco and got into Texas—taking our time,

3

you know—and I went into a secondhand bookstore. Someone must have disposed of an old library. And there was this book by a Eugene Shore. Well, just out of curiosity I bought it. I got it for 25 cents, wondering if by any chance the author could be you. Is it just a coincidence? It isn't you, is it?"

"I'm afraid it is, Mrs. Watson."

"Well, well, well! Imagine! A neighbor of mine. I'm glad I read the book."

"You read it? That was very kind of you, Mrs. Watson. Very neighborly. It's nice to know I have a reader here in town."

"But you know," she began hesitantly.

"Yes, Mrs. Watson?"

"Well, I suppose it comes down to this," she said dubiously. "I suppose I don't think like you think. Not about anything at all, Mr. Shore. I just don't think like you."

"Oh, I'm sure you don't," he said soothingly. "And what a good thing it is for you, Mrs. Watson." She thought she detected some good-humored disdain in his smile, and it worried her.

"Well, I can see you like my dog, anyway. Why don't you get a dog, Mr. Shore? There have been so many burglaries around here, and such strange people have started coming over the bridge. I'd feel very nervous without a dog. Your house may be the next one they break into."

"Oh, I don't think I have to get a dog," he said, laughing. "Burglars seem to understand that they should leave me alone." His was the only house on the street that hadn't been broken into. Maybe it was because he stayed up so late. The light burned all night in his library window. But Mrs. Watson, who had always thought the Shores, holding themselves so aloof, looked down at their neighbors, spitefully thought it would serve him right if his house was broken into and someone hit him on the head.

Mrs. Watson had the same thoughts every time she encountered Mr. Shore on the bridge—that is, until the middle of April that year. Then one of her neighbors telephoned and

4

asked if she had seen the *Evening World.* J. C. Hilton had mentioned Shore in his widely read column. Only part of the column was devoted to Shore, but there was also a picture. Hilton, in his "Man-About-Town" column, always printed a picture of the subject, whether it was a garbage collector or a society lady. The photographer had caught Shore crossing the bridge, wearing his new, spring, Cardin hat. Shore had looked up with an amused (or was it disdainful?) smile. Hilton wrote that he had stumbled on a novel by Eugene Shore, and because Shore was a local man, he had read the book. But the story had so exasperated him that he had hurled the book across the room. In doing so, he had knocked over a table lamp, and the lamp, he assured his readers, was worth a lot more than Shore's perverse book. His wife had liked the lamp and had bought it at a flea market in the country. He figured Shore at least owed him the price of the lamp.

"Well, there you are," Mrs. Watson said to her husband with considerable satisfaction and began telephoning her neighbors.

2

Shore's picture had appeared in the paper on the first really warm day after the April cold snap. That was the way it was in this city: cold, then suddenly everything was green in the hard sunlight, as if there were only two seasons. At the roof bar of the Park Plaza the doors to the terrace overlooking downtown had been flung open. In the new, bright sunlight the city seemed to be all trees. The terrace looked down on the university campus, the museum, and the park, although farther downtown were the towering new tombstone slabs and then the lake. Near the entrance to the terrace was a table where Al Delaney sat with his drinking companions. Passing Hilton's column in the *Evening World* around, they took turns laughing. The little man with the nervous eyes, the heavy sideburns, the bumptious manner, and the expensive plaid jacket, was Russ Myers, the television critic. He knew all about the great Russian poet, Mandelshtam. The balding man with the twisted grin, Ron Stasiak, went to all the Cannes film festivals, had written about them in *Life* magazine, and counted himself a friend of Ingmar Bergman. The handsome girl, Helena, who now was reading Hilton's column, was a sculptress who worked in iron and had lovely, long legs. Delaney had a little, black, spade beard and deep, soft, restless eyes. He drove a taxi three nights a week. The rest of his time he devoted to finishing up at the graduate school. These friends of his believed he was onto something and would soon make a big name for himself. As he saw it, his dissertation, which was on Norman Mailer, was just a step—as was the sinecure awaiting him at the university. The dissertation was to become the book that would make him famous. He often came to the hotel wearing his taxi cap, but with his beard and curling brown hair and elegant Spanish leather jacket, he looked like a prince down on his luck. No one who worked at the hotel told him to take off the cap. Al and his friends had a secret agreement, that they really belonged to a bigger world outside the town. Often he lectured them on Sartre, Marcuse, Borges, and Beckett. He knew about all the trends in the world's capitals, although he was the ony one who had never been abroad.

Al and his friends were laughing now but not at Shore. They weren't interested in him. Old Hilton was the butt of their jokes. Taking an idle glance at the Shore picture, Helena said: "The guy looks kind of cute. I like that hat. Something Irish about it. Silly old Hilton is such an ass man. Every day the ass man cometh. Yesterday he was kissing some rich woman's ass. Today he is kicking some poor local writer's ass." They had long ago agreed that Hilton was an old English joke on the town. Forty years ago Hilton had gone to England where he had hacked it out getting nowhere. Finally he had come home and conned an editor into believing that in London he had been a figure among figures.

"If you have to kick someone in the ass, if that's your way of life, who's better than a local writer nobody ever heard of?" Al said. For him it was the first time Shore's name had come up. "So what else is new today?" he said. Really, he was busy with his own affairs. April was the busiest month of the year at the graduate school. He had written brilliant final papers, and tomorrow was the day of his oral defense.

Al was the son of a successful hardware dealer. He had come out of the west with his good, casual clothes, black spade

8

beard, and challenging grin and had shown that he could take on the torturing graduate school in his spare time and lick it. His friends called him "The Champ." He always had a new girl in his bed, needed little sleep, and with a sudden, fierce light in his brown eyes got into short, quick fights in bars. He believed that his taxi-driving had kept him from going crazy under the pressure of the rigid discipline of the graduate school. Terrible things happened in his cab. A 17-year-old drug addict had tried to knife him because he had refused to take the boy to a place where he could get a fix. Old women quarreled with him about tips. A pretty hooker named Maybelle, a friend of his now, kept trying to do a deal. She offered him 40 percent of any John's fee if Al had recommended her, but if the John visited her a second time, the fee was all hers. Girls got drunkenly sick in his cab. Old thieves told him their troubles. Al kept track of these encounters in his journal. He was always saying to himself, *I want to know why.* He had a passion for understanding, based always on disciplined analysis.

He kept his journal in the top dresser drawer, under his shirts, in the big room in Mrs. Burnside's place on Monteith. Often he would amuse himself by analyzing the notes, trying to discover whether his experiences had any pattern that would give a meaning to his life. On one page he had written that it was shameful for a father to know nothing about his own son. Four years ago he had refused to go into the hardware business. He and his father quarreled, and Al had left home, wandering around the country until his father had written: "There may be worse things in the world than being a professor. Anyway, it helps keep you off the streets."

The hardware dealer, who had paid the rent on Al's room up until last January, didn't know about the taxi nor that Al was saving the taxi money for a trip to Europe. But last January, his father, while attending a convention came to town unexpectedly and telephoned Al from a downtown hotel to say he had the check for the three months' back rent. It was the night of the great snowstorm. It had been snowing all day and into the night; the city's snow-removal equipment had broken down. Al was having a party. Feeling good, he impulsively asked his father to come and meet his friends. Taxis were hard to get in the snowstorm; by the time Mr. J. C. Delaney arrived, it was nearly midnight, and everyone was a little drunk. He was a sober, dignified man, balding and with a high color. He wore a dark brown, double-breasted suit. Al's friends felt they should be as free with him as they were with Al. The hardware dealer learned about Al's taxi. He was willing to listen with respect to intellectual conversations among college students. But the girls kept saying "oh, shit," or "you're full of shit," or "that's absolute shit." Then he heard Maggie Symons, who was squatting on the floor at his feet, looking like a lovely waif, say: "All that crap about deep vaginal satisfaction, too! It is crap, you know." Mr. Delaney stood up with a silly, fixed smile. "Where's Al?" he asked nervously. But just then a man with iron-gray hair started a fight. Breaking it up, Al got hit on the head with a bottle and began to bleed. "Throw them all out," his father shouted. He couldn't understand why Al, mopping his head with a wet towel, wasn't also enraged. "They're all drunk," he said. "Take it easy," Al said. "It's just a party." Outraged, stiff-mouthed, staring as if Al were destroying everything he respected, the hardware dealer finally said: "Where's my coat?" He didn't wait for Al to call a taxi. Instead he fled into the snowstorm. And he didn't leave the check.

After the party broke up, Al sat drinking till dawn with Jake Fulton. He kept touching the cut on his head, but he was really wounded by his own surprise. "I'll never get another cent, but what really bothers me is that I thought I knew what went on in my father."

Since that night he had been living on what he could earn. He had had to give his taxi savings to Mrs. Burnside for the back rent.

The day after Shore's picture appeared in the Hilton column, Al had made his oral defense, and finished graduate school feeling the job was done and done in first-rate fashion. There had been a heavy shower, but now there was strong sunlight as he came on down the path toward the park. Pale and thin from living on hamburgers and cornflakes, his eyes full of nervous energy, he looked like a Jesus just out of the desert.

Suddenly he stopped, remembering, and turned, looking back at the college, filled with astonishment. "That nitpicking bastard," he said softly. "He could have ruined my whole career. I should have expected it from him."

He had known that Dr. Morton Hyland would be one of the committee of interrogators. Hyland was the biggest scholar and cultural figure in town, and students came from all over the continent to study his theories of literature and learn his system. Al had never been afraid of the false humility or the scholarship of this small, pudgy, sandy-haired man with short fingers and big, brown freckles on his forehead. But he couldn't have known that Dr. Hyland had eaten an overripe melon with toast for breakfast that morning and had discovered during the defense that his stomach was souring on him. Hyland had asked meanly, "What was the name of that Dublin hotel where the woman Joyce was to run off with worked?" The niggardly question made Al stare at Dr. Hyland. His mind went blank, but he wasn't in a panic. Staring at the four graying professional heads, then at their old tweed jackets and scruffy shoes, he found himself wondering why both professors and jazz musicians always wore scuffed-up shoes, and then he felt cold and overwhelmingly lonely. There was no sound but the beating of his own heart, and a voice, hardly his own, said: "You're nothing, Al. Nothing."

"Well," he said abruptly and walked out of the office. He went to the drinking fountain in the hall. His dissertation director, Dr. Steele, a grave and kindly man who had modeled his life on the seventeenth-century divines, came to him and said anxiously, "Are you alright, Delaney?" Al said calmly: "Of course I am, Dr. Steele. I'm merely getting a drink. I'm not phoning all the hotels in Dublin." He went back to the office and smiled at Dr. Hyland and answered the question.

But now, there on the path looking back, he wasn't smiling. He was astonished, remembering that awful, lonely

11

moment when he had not known himself. He swayed a little, not so much seeing as feeling the other students hurrying by him to lunch. A shaft of sunlight shot through clouds high over the government building to the south, and the greenness of the sunlit, wet grass and the glitter on the wet tree leaves came so painfully close that he shivered. Then the whole picture in front of him shook, and he held onto himself, stunned and quivering. Then with relief, he recognized the feeling; it was like being gloriously drunk. All the nervous tensions from the strain and lack of sleep and concentration had blasted his imagination. It took him only a moment to realize he was alright. He was Al Delaney who had just had another big day. He loafed proudly down the crescent around the park to his fine, big room on Monteith.

It was a short, dead-end street. Some of the old brick houses had been sandblasted and made into town houses with expensive apartments. Mrs. Burnside, a widow, had taken a hundred dollars from her husband's insurance money; now the front of her house was sandblasted too, and she had rigged up four rooms with kitchenettes. Al had the second-floor room at the front of the house. When he came in Mrs. Burnside, having heard his step, opened her door. She was a big, deep-breasted woman with a pile of graying blonde hair who had a pinched nerve in her neck. The surgical collar she wore made her look like the first female bishop. "How did you do, Al?" she called.

"No trouble at all."

"Always the boss, eh?"

"This time, anyway."

"That's it, then?"

"Just the book now."

"I was getting myself something to eat. How about a bowl of soup? I'll bring it to you."

"What kind of soup?"

"My onion soup, Al."

"Great," he said, going up the stairs. "You're a beautiful woman."

The big room was neat and clean with nicely balanced

prints of abstract impressionist paintings on the walls, and the books in their shelves were in an orderly arrangement. His papers, too, were in a neat pile on the desk. Slumping into the chair at the desk, he stared at the bed until Mrs. Burnside brought him the bowl of hot soup.

"Ah, this is good," he said. When she had gone he sipped the soup, but he could hardly lift the spoon. His eyes were on the bed again. Finally he got up slowly, dropped on the bed, and soon was sound asleep. The ringing of the phone in the hall woke him, and he staggered out into the hall. "Yeah," he mumbled into the mouthpiece.

"Los Angeles calling. Here you are."

"Yeah?"

"Al. Is that you, Al? It doesn't sound like you." It was his brother Dave who had left home and learned the bartender's trade so he could go where he wanted to go and make good money. "Do something for me, will you, Al?" Dave said.

"Sure, Dave. What's up?"

"Here's the situation." Dave told him that another bartender—an older, superior man everyone in the trade looked up to—had found out where Dave was from and invited him home, where he showed Dave his collection of the writings of a man named Eugene Shore. He was showing them to Dave, he said, because Dave had talked about Shore's home town. Dave, who didn't know who the hell this Shore was, had lied and said his brother was a friend of Shore's and could get Shore to autograph a couple of books. Would Al do this for him? Would he get them down airmail so he could give them to his bartender friend?

"Wait a minute. Did you say Shore?"

"Yeah, Eugene Shore. Have you got it?"

"I've got it. Hey, wait a minute. What the hell is this, Dave?" He thought at first that he was confused or still half asleep. Then he got mad. "For God's sake, Dave. I'm still asleep. You wake me up with this?"

"Please, Al, my prestige is at stake."

"Oh, hell, Dave," he groaned. "Okay, okay." But as he

hung up he thought. Good God, this is going to cost me money. He didn't want to go back to sleep, so he washed his face and combed his hair. It was five o'clock when he went out to a bookstore.

There had been another shower, but the sun was out, drying the sidewalk. Down the street some people had gathered on the muddy lawn of one of the unrenovated houses. A child in blue pajamas lay flat on the ground, motionless, staring at the ring of faces above him. "Up there," a stout woman said, pointing. "He fell out that window. His mother's up the street somewhere. Why the hell is she always up the street?" "Are you alright?" Al asked, squatting down. Not a word came from the child. "Don't touch him, mister," they all said. A doctor had been called. The child whimpered and closed his eyes. While Al was wondering what to do, an elegant girl—black-haired, hatless, self-assured—came out of one of the new apartments, heading for a small, red car parked at the curb. "Hello there, Lisa," Al called. He had known Lisa Tolen casually in graduate school. Now she was a researcher at one of the television stations. She had been delivering material to her producer.

"Al, that poor kid is shivering," she said. Kneeling down, she talked gently to the child. "Oh dear, he'll catch pneumonia lying there in the mud," she said. She touched the child's legs and moved his fingers. "I'm sure nothing's broken. This is ridiculous. Come on, son," and she lifted the child. "Hey, don't do that. You're not supposed to touch him," a man called. She carried him to the house. Al opened the door, and they went into the front room where there was a couch. Putting the child down, she knelt beside him, soothing him and smiling, until the doctor arrived. "Who moved the boy?" he asked. While he was scolding Lisa, the mother burst in and stood listening, then she berated Lisa until the ambulance came.

A cop who had come with the ambulance took Lisa by the arm. "You should leave things in the hands of the proper authorities, miss." He was ready to lead her to the door. She stared coldly at the hand on her arm, then looked at the cop. Al quickened. He didn't know what he expected as her head went

14

back and her eyes flashed. Whatever it was in her that had moved her to carry the child was in this sudden silent violent confrontation with the cop. Her eyes were slashing. The cop, unnerved, dropped her arm uneasily and went out.

"You know the boy is all right," Lisa said to the ambulance driver, "unless the doctor thinks he should have pneumonia." As the doctor examined him, the child reached for Lisa's hand. The doctor could find nothing wrong: a bruise on the knee, a big welt on his hip; that was all. "Just the same," he said testily, "he shouldn't have been moved."

"Oh crap," Lisa said.

The ambulance and doctor left. The child still held onto Lisa's hand. When she tried to release his fingers, he started to cry. The mother, humiliated, burst out angrily: "Go, for God's sake, go." She showed Lisa and Al to the door. Outside Lisa turned to Al with a charming, helpless smile, "Well, I guess that's the way I am."

"I'm always good with cops. Can I give you a lift?"

"Drop me off at Britnell's?"

As they walked to the car he was ill at ease. She hadn't been around the university for a year, and he remembered when he had first met her, how he had shied away. She was supposed to have money and be clever and hard to handle. "How is it we never talked before?" she asked suddenly.

"You weren't around."

"I don't think I liked your name. Al! No. Al's a loser's name."

"It is? Well, too bad you're not English."

"English?"

"An Englishman told me that in his country I'd be called Bert."

"Okay, Bert."

"It's no good, though. My name's not Albert. It's Alexander."

"Alexander the Great, eh?"

"That's me."

"So I've heard," she said, smiling as she got into the car.

When they had driven out of the dead-end street she asked: "What are you getting at Britnell's? What are you reading?"

"Eugene Shore."

"Shore! Doesn't he live around here?"

"It's a funny story," he said and told her about his brother and the bartender. The bartender was probably a book collector. Those guys, all nuts, liked obscure, underdog writers. A traffic light changed, and Lisa stopped the car. Al turned to her idly, joking about collectors. She listened, her eyes on the light. He turned away, then, mystified, turned back to her quickly, the expression on her face taking him by surprise. He had had a glimpse of her in a strange stillness. His surprise didn't come from a sexual feeling; no, in this stillness she was far removed from him. But he had the feeling that somehow the bits of his life had suddenly come together for a moment but only for a moment. Catching himself he drew back, thinking: there I go again. The brightness of the world, like it hit me on the path, got me again. Everything bright and close. He wondered if it was the same excitement he had gotten watching her confront the cop.

They were nearly to Britnell's bookstore, but he couldn't let her go, feeling like this. Yet he couldn't buy her a drink and pay for the Shore books too; he didn't have the money. He resented Eugene Shore. It was absurd that a man he neither knew nor cared about should get in the way. So much for Mr. Shore, he thought, and turned to Lisa. "Let's skip the bookstore," he said. "Let's go to the Park Plaza and have a drink."

"Why not do both?"

"My father always said, 'my son, do one thing at a time.'"

"Okay," she said, as if she knew exactly how much money he had in his pocket.

They drove to the corner of the two hotels, the museum, and the broad avenue leading down to the colleges, parked the car, and started toward the elevator for the roof bar. But Al remembered that his friends might be up there, and they would get in the way. So he suggested that they go to the first-floor lounge. In the corner in the shadows, they were by themselves.

16

She took off her coat. In a black dress she leaned back against the red leather, she with a Bloody Mary and he with a Scotch.

Al began to feel his way into her life, his eyes saying, *Who are you?* He asked what had been happening to her, and she said easily, "Nothing of any consequence."

The intense curiosity in his eyes flattered her. Shrugging, she supposed, that her life had been somewhat disordered, probably more than his. If he remembered—but of course there was no reason why he should—she had taken a course in psychology and then, bored, had switched to the arts college. And she had walked out on that too. She could afford to switch around. Her father, a rich broker living in the Bahamas, sent her a check every three months. She skied and played tennis.

How was he at tennis? She was willing to bet she could beat him. As for her job at the television station, it was just a job, sometimes interesting, sometimes dull. Her boss, a nice, shy, married man, seemed a little afraid of her.

"Oh, I'm sure he is," Al said.

"Oh, that's cruel, Al. No one's afraid of me."

"That cop was."

"Are you a cop?"

"Not quite, not until I'm a professor."

"Professor!"

"What's the matter with that?"

"It's well, a little withdrawn, shall we say?"

"Look, Lisa," he said, "500 years ago I might have been a monk, poring over manuscripts, working my way up among the big theologians, all those artful guys who hang angels by the short hairs. Now I'm in another, bigger, richer church. We're everywhere. Five hundred years ago no prince worth his salt would go to the toilet without his spiritual advisor. Now no big executive, no politician, is without his academic. Everybody has his Kissinger. You call this withdrawn?"

"Al, you're in literature. Who cares about the language?"

"Who sets the tone of the time, the trend? McLuhan, mouthpiece for Madison Avenue, just a professor who used to write about Tennyson, all those guys talking McLuhan's talk.

Kennedy, Trudeau, Nixon—you want to know why their speeches sound like first-year papers in political science? It's because they're written by guys who did some English, guys who don't have to know anything. All Nixon wants is a certain tone."

"You know something, Al," she said, studying him gravely, "All around me are confused men who don't know where they are going." She had been twisting with her long, strong fingers one of the little paper napkins under her drink. Impulsively, she said: "I kind of like being here with you." She took his hand and looked at the palm and held it, frowning.

"What's there?" Al asked.

"That's the lifeline. Everybody should know about lifelines."

"I don't."

"It's quite a life you've got there."

"So, tell me more."

"No, I don't think I will," and she frowned.

"Why don't you tell me?"

"Tell all I know?"

"Come on, Lisa. A guy's got to know where he's going."

"What's the use? You think you know."

"Well, I've got to believe in something."

"What do you believe in, Al?"

"Well," and he paused, looking at her gravely, "I believe I'll have another drink."

She blinked and then laughed. It was a laugh he had always wanted to hear from a woman—deep and husky, a warm, dark laugh coming out of her whole being. When she got her breath she said: "Where did you get that?"

"I'm a scholar," he said. "It's the first principle of scholarship that you take it where you find it."

"Alright, scholar, what're you doing this summer?"

"Driving a taxi. Finishing my book. Maybe going to Europe."

"I love Europe," she said. "What's your book about?"

Shrugging, he said, "The big contemporary personality, a lot about Mailer."

18

"Oh, Mailer," she said, smiling. "I see."

"See what?"

"I get the hang of you. Mailer's good fun, isn't he?" and she laughed. "Are you going to make your own march on the Pentagon?"

"Look," he said—and he was earnest with her—"I'm not some nineteenth-century reactionary taking a wonderful, detached view of culture. Not on your life. You know, in football, what they call the play along the line, where all the holes are made for the fancy Dans to run through and look good. They call it the pit, where you take all the punches, all the stuff they can throw at you. That's where I want to be—take it all into me, make something out of it, something bigger for myself." While he was saying all this, for all his flow of words, he was still trying to analyze her better, waiting expectantly. Her eyes sparkled. She had a long neck and little mole on her left cheek, and when she nodded, her tongue touched her lips.

The bar was filling up. Single men—slick and groomed in expensive business suits—brokers and ad men and journalists came in. "Hello, Lisa," two or three called. Al, watching her smile and wave, was a little irritated. He wouldn't deign to turn. Finally, as she sat settled back against the red leather in the luxurious snuggling droop of her body, he told himself that she was all sexual grace. It was there in her movements, delicate, suggestive. She was able to make him feel that she held him in her inner eye, smiling to herself. Coolly and analytically he concluded that the expression on her face, which had fascinated him in the car, could have been one of these effortless sexual graces. She might even have been using it knowingly on him. It's all sexual charm, he thought—and there was nothing wrong with that.

"You know something, Al? You're not like I thought you were. I used to think you were a bit of a showboat. Yes, I did. But I like talking to you. People don't talk to each other in this town. No one really tells anything. No one wants to know." With her hand going out to his, she said gently: "You shouldn't let yourself get so run-down, Al."

"You don't know me, Lisa. I go up and down like a yo-yo."

19

"I'm hungry. Aren't you?"

"Food?" he asked awkwardly.

"How about some food at my place?"

"Come on, then."

After he had paid the waiter and they were out into the late sunlight, she said, taking his arm: "You need someone to look after you."

Lisa's place was only a five-minute drive from the university, on Walmer Road, a street of trees and big old houses broken up into apartments. She had the upper floor. A chestnut tree stood in front of the house. In Lisa's disordered, white-walled living room there wasn't a picture or print on the walls.

She gave him vodka and some cold cuts. All the drink, plus the week's strain, made him warm and drowsy. "Ah, Lisa," he sighed. "You and me," and he put his arm around her, imagining that he was leading her slowly along the hall to her bedroom. She humored him, steadying him when he lurched. "Well now, Lisa," he said, smiling wisely as he sat on the bed. But then he rolled over, sound asleep.

At dawn the garbage men bouncing cans in the alley awoke him. She was in bed beside him. His hand went to her. "Take it easy," she said and got up and made him some coffee. She was wearing a short, blue nightgown. They said nothing. When he had finished his coffee, she took the cup, put it on the dresser, and then got in bed with him.

Her lovemaking surprised him. Her hands, her hips, were a shy, gentle caress, helping him to know her. His mind swimming, he murmured: "Lisa, what is it?"

"Nothing, nothing, Al," she whispered.

He dozed beside her. When he woke up, she was at her dressing table, still in her nightgown, combing her hair. As she put down the comb she lifted her head, her face caught by the morning light. Al stiffened, mute and dazzled by some sense of wholeness, for there she was again for him—in her stillness, transporting him somewhere beyond himself. Quickening, he reached toward her, as if in his lovemaking he hadn't touched her at all.

20

"Lisa . . . "

"Oh, you're awake."

"Oh, I'm wide awake."

"You don't have to get up," she said casually. "You can sleep all day. You need to, I'd say. I'll pick up those books at Britnell's. Go back to sleep." She took her dress and went into the bathroom.

He listened to her moving around, going from the bathroom to the kitchen. Lying back, closing his eyes, he searched for something he thought he had seen in her face. If he went closer to her in her stillness, would the effect be broken, the effect inside himself? A girl who could give him this sudden sense of harmony—surely she had some view of her own life. Something moving, something significant, must have happened to her. There had to be a structure behind it. How aware was she of herself? Could she explain her effect on him? Of course not. Could he explain it to himself? He knew he had always been good at measuring the achieved effects of painters and writers. Information. Get all the information. He had the tool he trusted: analysis. He had never had any patience with mysteries. Everything could be explained. That's why he kept his journal, his notes about himself. All his training made him reject mysteries.

3

A sound in the kitchen woke him, and he knew that Lisa, home from work, was letting him sleep. When he got up he saw that his clothes had been moved. They were in her bedroom closet. Her dresses had been pushed along the bar that held the coat hangers. His folded pants were on a coat hanger, too.

He took a shower, dressed quickly, and was tying his shoelaces, sitting on the side of the bed, when she came in with a parcel. Her simple yellow dress looked expensive.

"Hello, there."

"You're an angel; you let me sleep."

"You look better now," she said, opening the parcel. "There, the two books for your brother." She had an amused smile. "I figured I cost you the price of these two books. As a matter of fact, I had a hell of a time getting them. My own bookstore didn't have any books by Shore. Had to send over to the publisher's warehouse. Here you are, professor."

"Well, thanks," he said awkwardly. "You didn't need to do this, Lisa." Still embarrassed, he laughed. "Damn it all, I've got to get them autographed. What a bore."

"All you have to do is look Shore up in the phone book," she said.

"That's true. Well, I guess I should be getting home."

"What's the rush? Meeting someone?"

"Not exactly."

"I thought you might be having something to eat with me."

"Lisa—I should take you out to dinner."

"I'll take a rain check," she said, smiling. She knew he didn't have the money.

While she cooked dinner, Al looked up Eugene Shore in the phone book. Lisa knew the neighborhood, she said. She'd had a girl friend who'd lived near there. It was only 15 minutes away.

Watching her move around, Al smiled to himself, wondering if she was all generosity. She asked him about his place, and he told her that he was very comfortable with Mrs. Burnside who would let him borrow money. Now, of course, he would have to give full time to taxi-driving. Then he told her about his dream of finishing the dissertation on Mailer and getting money from the taxi for his European trip. Frowning, as if she were already deeply involved in his plans, she said she couldn't see why he couldn't forget about the taxi and concentrate on finishing up the book and being rid of it.

"Hey, lady, I've got to live," he said. "I've got to pay the rent."

"Oh, that! Yes." There was always a place to sleep and type, wasn't there? For that matter, he could use her place. It sounded like an idle observation.

He thought she was joking, because, while she talked, she had moved into the dining room and was setting the table with some lovely little Italian place mats. Before sitting down, he called Shore. A woman who said she was Mrs. Shore told him her husband was out for dinner but that she expected him home about 9:30.

When he told Lisa, sitting with her at the table, he thought she wasn't much interested, yet 20 minutes later, giving him his coffee, she said: "Why don't we take a chance and go over there?" He agreed enthusiastically. The ride would keep her with him, and he was curious about sitting beside her again in that little red car where he had felt her strange stillness.

24

It took only ten minutes to reach the Shore neighborhood which at that hour, with the street lights shining through the tall trees and a bright moon rising, was like an island park in the downtown city, and as quiet as a park, too. The rumble of the city was beyond the ravine. Lisa parked the car near the footbridge and they sauntered up the street past the wide lawns which looked even greener in the night light.

"There. That must be the Shore place," Al said. It was big and solid, a simple, vine-covered house. "Hmm. Looks like money," he said. "I can hear the coupon-clipping already. He can't be a real writer. What's he doing living here?"

A man was coming up the street toward them, a solid figure, walking like a man intent on appearing dignified and sober, while swerving a little and occasionally holding onto his hat. Passing Al and Lisa, he continued on, self-absorbed, controlling himself beautifully, lurching only a little when he turned into the Shore house. At the door he fumbled for his key.

"My God," Al said. "That's Shore."

"Are you sure?"

"It's the same hat he had on in the picture."

"What picture? I didn't see any picture."

"That crazy Hilton column,"

"I didn't read it."

"The guy's a little drunk. He's apt to say anything," Al said reluctantly. "He may ask how I liked his books."

"Tell him you loved them."

"Goddamn it, I really resent this. It's belittling."

"Here, give them to me," she said, laughing, and took the books. With him trailing behind, she went up the steps and rang the bell. Al hung back in the shadow by the wisteria-covered pillar. Shore must have still been in the vestibule, taking off his hat, for the door was opened immediately. Behind him they could see a hall leading into a wide well with a staircase. Mrs. Shore, a handsome, gray-haired woman in a black dress, was crossing from the winding stairs. In the vestibule light Shore looked a little flushed. He had soft blue eyes and great natural composure.

"Yes?"

"Mr. Shore?" Lisa said.

"Yes."

"This is presumptuous, I know," she said, putting on her breathless charming tone and warm smile. "But we saw you going in, and it looked like a great chance to have you autograph these two books. Would you, please, Mr. Shore—?"

"Books of mine?" he asked. "What is this?" He tried to make out Al's face in the shadow of the pillar. Turning, he switched on the veranda light and again appraised them. In this town young people did not come to his door asking him to autograph books. His whole expression seemed to say: *What is this? What are you up to? Who sent you here?* But, because he was a polite man, he stepped aside with a courtly bow, ready to invite them in. Again hesitating, he stiffened. His eyes grew wary as if he were hearing a voice saying, *Don't let these strangers in,* and he suddenly shifted his body. He was back blocking the door again. "Why these two books?" he said, taking them from Lisa.

"They're to go to California," Lisa said, hoping to flatter him. "You have an admirer in Los Angeles."

"Oh, I see," he said gravely. He had obviously guessed that neither Lisa nor Al had read the books. Suddenly he stepped out on the veranda. He closed the door behind him and gave them an amused little grin. But when he had stepped forward, Lisa, who was directly under the light, had to take a step backward. Now the light fell on her face. Taking a pen from his pocket, Shore glanced at her. Then he gave her another quick surprised look. Al wondered whether Shore had recognized her.

"Have we met somewhere?" Lisa asked.

"Well, no . . . "

"I thought . . . "

"Yes, I know." Smiling to himself, he opened one of the books and began to autograph the title page. "Its alright," he said, as if she had admitted that she knew nothing about his work. "You don't need to bother reading them. You're in them."

26

"Me?" she said. "Really?"

"Really."

"As what?" Al asked, stepping forward.

"As what?" Shore repeated, turning to Al. "Well, it would depend. I don't know how you see things." He finished the autographing and handed the books to Lisa. "There you are. Thank you and good night."

"Thank you, Mr. Shore. Good night."

"Good night, Mr. Shore."

He had already closed the door. They walked slowly to the sidewalk.

"Well, that was something," she said, stopping, by herself in her thoughts.

"What was that all about?"

"Search me."

"I thought for a minute he was going to ask us in."

"So did I."

"You could be in his books!" Al snorted. "Like anybody'd want to be. What a corny line. Come on! He should be a book salesman. Maybe he is."

"Yeah," she said, still looking back at the house. She tried to laugh. "He must have thought he had met me somewhere, don't you think?"

"Oh, hell," Al said. "Come on."

"Al, I just thought of something. Mailer's okay, with his giant jumps at the moon. Maybe he *is* the man in the moon. Maybe it suits you."

"Thanks."

"That's not what I mean, though. I mean, a hundred guys are writing about Mailer. You're not only taking on Mailer, you're taking on all of those guys. Why not look into Shore? He might be interesting."

"What for? Shore's a nobody. I'm no Los Angeles bartender." He snorted again.

"Alright. It was just a hunch. Hey, look, there he is."

A light had come on in the room to the right of the front door. The shades weren't drawn. It was the library; the walls were lined with bookshelves. They could see Shore go into the

27

room and sit down in a rocking chair. He began to rock slowly, staring out of the window, far over the ravine and far beyond the wall of apartments on the other side. He rocked back and forth, back and forth. Al couldn't take his eyes off him. This man, this local author—all presumption—in one quick glance had placed Lisa in his own little scheme of things. No mystery about her for him, sitting there rocking in his impassive stillness.

"Who the hell does he think he is?" Al said irritably. "Come on, Lisa. We got what we wanted. Let's go."

"Where?" she said.

"Well—"

"We might as well go back to my place," she said quickly. "I don't feel like going out any place," as if he had just suggested a choice of elegant places. They got in the car.

At her place Al felt almost shy, watching her. Only last night he had had her in his arms. Now he felt that last night, in his exhaustion and excitement, he hadn't really known her. He had no real awareness of her body. But she was here now, in a loose, blue-and-yellow, silk Chinese coat, beside him on the couch. While he pretended to concentrate on the music she was playing, he was shaken by this unfamiliar shyness and curiosity about her body. Last night didn't count. This feeling came in moments when, missing a breath, he heard his heart beat heavily.

Lisa turned to him with a thoughtful smile and asked if he wanted a drink. He didn't. Neither did she, she said. They got up, kissed gently, and went into the bedroom where she immediately turned off the light. "Lisa," he protested, "I want to look at you!" "No, tonight I want it to be in the dark," she said. They got in bed. His curiosity unsatisfied, Al tried to picture all of her through the exploring touch of his hands, following her every line with his hands. Saying nothing, she opened her arms, taking him to her with a loving, warm ease. Sometimes little snorts came from her. Finally, when she could only be inert and still, she curled up beside him, her fingers going through his hair and his beard. She laughed softly. "You

28

have this—what do they call it?—this animal craving for me, and I, shameless little hussy that I am, seem to have the same thing about you. Ah, you're beautiful, Al."

"You said I was a showboat."

"I said I *used* to think you were a showboat."

"Come on now, you still do."

"Oh, go on."

"No, it came up again."

"When?"

"Coming out of Shore's place."

"How?"

"You said that Mailer suits me."

"Al, I said I didn't mean that."

"You know what I think you meant?"

"What?"

"Mailer is a kind of showboat, so he would appeal to me."

"Oh, Al." She laughed, her head still down on the pillow, then she murmured drowsily: "What did that man Shore do to get under your skin?"

"Shore's nothing. It was you."

"Alright, Al," she murmured into the pillow. "I'm under your skin here, and it feels so warm and good." He thought she was falling asleep. His eyes were getting used to the room's darkness. A narrow strip of light came in from between the window drapes. It seemed to be widening.

"What are you thinking about now?"

"Your face."

"What's wrong with my face?"

"Nothing; it does things to me."

"Just my face?"

"That I don't know," he said, his eyes on the strip of light at the window. "It's kind of complicated, I guess." He laughed softly. "Can the face of someone close to you tell you something about yourself? I mean, well, carry it on a little. Yesterday the mayor's picture was in the newspapers, eh? That dull ordinary face with the accountant's little moustache must surely tell the story of this town. Right? Well, whatever you make of

29

life must surely show in the face of someone who loves you as much as it shows in your own face. Have you thought of that, Lisa? They say a man and woman who live together for a long time find that life comes to mean the same thing for them, and they begin to look alike."

"Yeah," she mumbled drowsily. "Stick around, Al, and we'll get to look alike." Then she was asleep.

When he awoke in the morning she had gone to work. He got up and drew the window drapes. Across the alley was a balcony on which a woman was sunning herself in the bright sunlight. She had a thin disappointed face, he thought. Her husband's whole life probably showed in her face. Then, as he pondered, smiling to himself and rubbing his head, he suddenly knew that he couldn't leave here no matter how comfortable he had been with Mrs. Burnside. He couldn't leave Lisa's place.

4

Al moved in with Lisa, into her spare bedroom. When his stuff came from Mrs. Burnside's, he put his desk near the window that overlooked the next door balcony and his book shelves on the wall to the left of the desk. The bed that had been in this room was really a couch. He put his prints on the wall over the couch. His typewriter went on a little table beside the desk. The white bareness of the walls, the same white that was on the walls of all the rooms, bothered him. His working space should be apart from all this whiteness, he thought, so he asked Lisa if he could paint the room.

He painted one wall a soft brown and the other three a light green.

He had his special clothes for writing—an old sweater and a pair of brown corduroys. The sweater had once been a beautiful thing of red-and-white, barber pole stripes. If he had to go out to the library, he would put on his fancy jacket and comb his hair and beard carefully. But as soon as he was home again he put on the old sweater. He would be in it when Lisa came home from work. He liked getting to the top of the stairs at the sound of the front door opening so he could see her face lifting to him under the hall light.

After dinner she would offer to retype the pages he had done during the day. He came to believe that he had made a mistake letting her do this. He would think so every time he saw her sitting at his desk with her big horn-rimmed reading glasses on, frowning as she read, her face full of intelligence, then looking at him and saying with a slow smile: "Anyway, Al, you certainly have a wide-ranging, free mind," as if she really thought he was wasting his time. Then, knowing she didn't give a damn about Mailer, he remembered her saying: "Mailer's right for you." Night after night when she was typing he heard this voice and tried to laugh it off. He knew she would pretend to be astonished. But now it was as if they were struggling over an attitude she had toward him that had been revealed in that ridiculous, phony, undignified visit to that man Shore. His attitude, as he imagined it, wounding his pride, struck at his whole view of himself. He wanted to smile and say: "Just who do you think you are to be taking this attitude toward me?" His half-amused, half-resentful curiosity began to gnaw at him. In little ways, such as talking over coffee with her, he searched into the corners of her life. His curiosity and questioning smile showed his need to be sure of her again. She told him with her eyes that he should not be taking her to pieces, that his dreadful analytical habit should not be used on her. She told it to him with her little laugh when they were in bed, lying in the dark and his fingers wandered lightly over her breasts and throat while he questioned her about her life.

"What are you after, Al?"

"You," he said, laughing softly.

Trying to laugh too, she said, "Alright. Right from the beginning. Here goes." She had been a Caesarian baby; she had never known her mother. She had gone to a convent school. Her father, who had married again, speculated in real estate in Nassau. For months at a time he would be out of the country, and when he returned she would fling herself at him, mad for his affection, for he could have such warmth, such a flow of gentle words. Finally he had settled in Nassau and taken a third young wife. Evidently each wife had to be younger. While he

32

remained far away and hidden, her affection for him had deepened, which was something she didn't understand. He grew rich, and sent her money faithfully.

"Even my name, Tolen," she said. "I began to distrust it. Where did I come from? What was my real background? Is there anything more you want to know, Al?" Again the little laugh in the dark. He was sure she knew that he wasn't satisfied.

"Alright. Was I ever in love? Is that it?" She told him she had had three lovers—a crazy painter who had left his wife, an advertising man who pretended his whole world was the theater, and a young director with whom she had played tennis and skied. She had a weakness for loaning money because she liked creating the surprise and sudden warmth in people. Suddenly she curled around Al, spoon fashion, and in this domestic position, whispered: "Why do these things matter now? They explain nothing about me. The important thing is, I feel that we can be at home with each other, do things for each other. Isn't that the way it should be?"

"Yeah, that should be the thing."

"And all these silly things I tell you—"

"No, those things bring you closer, Lisa."

"Oh, come on, Al." Then she sighed. "It's too bad, too. You know, Al, you had a great trick going for you."

"A trick?"

"Yeah. Sometimes I'd catch an expression on your face after I had caught you looking at me, and I'd have the lovely feeling that you had just been told everything you'd ever need to know. Oh, well, I'm sleepy. Good night, Al."

When he was sure she was sound asleep, he got up quietly, went into his room, and took his journal out of the desk drawer. There were the pages filled with all the crazy stuff about his life. But the one page entitled "Lisa" was still blank. As he stared at the blank page with a bemused smile, he could almost hear her little laugh.

5

In the late afternoon he came down the path by the museum and into the park, hurrying because it had clouded up and looked like rain. Cutting across the park, he came along by the government buildings, down and over to the Four Seasons. Then, standing at the entrance at exactly five o'clock, he saw her crossing the road. In her red suit she ducked through the five o'clock traffic, trying to look both ways at the same time, her long black hair swinging across her face. At this hour the lounge was crowded with regulars, the television and public relations people and journalists.

They all knew Lisa, but Al never felt at ease with them. "Al, just a minute," Lisa said, "there's poor Mirabelle," and she left the table and embraced a plump blonde, a researcher she worked with, who had just gotten out of the hospital. Mirabelle had blacked out while standing on a street corner and had cut her head badly.

Left alone, Al looked around. At the next table were three young men in expensive suits, their hair styled. They were reading newspapers and talking. Al was sure he heard, "Yeah, Shore . . . Eugene Shore. . . ." He got up and went to the lobby newsstand, got the *Evening World,* and came back to his table. On the second page was a big picture of Shore, wearing his Cardin hat at a rakish angle. "Good God," Al said. The whole page was given over to Shore—and no wonder!

The internationally celebrated critic, Starkey Kunitz, had written an essay on Shore—a long essay—the lead essay in the *New York Review of Books.* But that wasn't what the fuss was about. It seemed that Kunitz had belittled Shore's hometown. Kunitz said that no one in the town apparently had ever had the wit or judgment to show any appreciation of this unique figure, a man who had lived there for years. The *Evening World* was making a big thing of the insult. On the page were short interviews with local people. Dr. Hyland was given a signed column in which he dealt with both Kunitz and Shore.

"I'll be damned," Al said, shaken. He had the greatest respect for Kunitz. No one deserved more respect. Al gulped down his drink. Still rattled, he waved at Lisa until he got her eye, then pointed to the paper on the table and hurried to the newsstand to get another copy so they could both read the long story at the same time. When he came back, she was at the table, absorbed in her reading. They said nothing to each other as they read. There were many quotations from Kunitz who, in his forceful, lucid prose, announced his discovery of a master who ought to be read wherever the English language was spoken. "But who is the man who wrote these books?" Kunitz asked. "What do we know about him? What do any of his fellow townsmen know about him?" It was in this quotation that Kunitz belittled the town. He expressed astonishment that an artist of Shore's sensibility and sharp intelligence had been able to go on living year after year in a big, prosaic, commercial town, and there was no evidence that anyone there had ever appreciated his distinction.

Then there was a column of interviews with professors, lawyers, and neighbors of Shore's. Honestly and without any envy, they said they could not believe that Shore was such a unique personality. Why, the man had been seen around town every day! It was as if they had been told they had known only an imposter. Some said that Kunitz was fatuous in trying so loftily to put Shore above the town's taste. The best short interview was with Dean Prendergast, retired and working on Henry James. He confessed a past admiration for Kunitz. Now he pointed out that, while Kunitz might be the voice from Mount Sinai, he should have had the grace to come to town and look around. He could have seen the new theaters. He could have looked at the Civic Ballet or visited the museum with its splendid Chinese collection, or the Science Center. Above all, it might have been very rewarding for Mr. Kunitz if he had walked across the university campus and encountered Dr. Morton Hyland taking his brisk walk, for surely a man of Kunitz's stature would recognize that Dr. Hyland, in his Oxford lectures, had made himself, at the very least, the equal of Kunitz. Not much was said by the old dean about Shore's work or about Shore himself. A footnote following the interview with the dean said: "See editorial on page 6." Al quickly turned the page.

The editorial took the dean's tone. "Be that as it may about Eugene Shore . . ." and then they scolded Kunitz. Never had Kunitz got such a scolding. The editorial called attention to the remarks of Dr. Hyland, a man, they said, of unimpeachable balance and authority.

Hyland's column was accompanied by a picture of him. He had managed to look very theological, writing that in the time available, he had given two or three of the Shore books some careful scrutiny, and while it was true that the work had some merit, Shore was essentially a minor talent with no real sense of mythopoeia and was therefore quite outside the perennial stream in literature. An outsider almost dangerously wrongheaded! He could never make up his mind whether his women were whores or saints. Warming up, the doctor scolded Kunitz for his crankiness and for trying to put Shore above the town's cultural level. There were two or three local poets, Hyland wrote, whom he would like to thrust under the Kunitz nose. It was true that in his declining years Kunitz had been looking around for underdogs to champion, yet it was extremely unlikely that there would be any revival of the alleged Shore masterpieces.

"Old pope Hyland rides again," Al said, turning to Lisa. He was trying to take something out on Hyland, but it wasn't working. She sipped her drink, waiting for him to finish reading. He started in again, looked at her carefully, waited, then went to the bottom of the page where Fagin, the *Evening World*'s popular columnist, told with the amusing, candid detail that had won him his following how he had taken a cameraman with him to interview Shore and how the Shores' housekeeper, upon opening the door, listened to his request, retired for a minute, then returned, saying coldly: "Mr. Shore does not give interviews. When he is interviewed he interviews himself." And she closed the door. Fagin reported that he and the photographer had stood on the sidewalk, hoping that Shore would come out, and the photographer, looking up at the house, said mockingly: "So Mr. Shore doesn't give interviews? Well, I don't see any crowd here banging on his door. Who the hell does he think he is?"

"Well," Al said, putting down the paper.

"That's an odd thing," Lisa said. "That crack from the photographer. That's just what you said, Al."

"What?"

" 'Who the hell does he think he is?' "

"Come on, now, Lisa," he protested. "It was the way he looked at you, talked to you, as if he knew he had you in his pocket and was giving you a consoling little pat on the behind."

"I know." Then she laughed. "But don't say I didn't give you a tip."

"Oh, sure."

"No, I go by my hunches," she said, sitting back, off by herself, having thoughts he couldn't fathom. Then as her eyes met his, her expression changed. The gentle sympathy behind her slow smile embarrassed him. He was sure she had been thinking of Al and his drinking companions, all pretending to

38

be so aware of what was going on in the world, and of him lecturing them on the important figures in the great capitals, how it had turned out that he, like all others, couldn't recognize a real talent right under his nose, and had to let Kunitz come in and tell him to read Shore. The embarrassment deepened.

"I like that bitchy little laugh, Lisa."

"I didn't know I was laughing."

"The truth is, I amuse you, don't I?"

"Oh, you can be amusing, sure," she said lightly. "A man who can't amuse a woman is a terrible drag."

"No, that's not it."

"Oh? What is, then?"

"All along I've amused you, haven't I? Right from the beginning, you've found me amusing."

"Oh, Al. Come on."

"Just don't think I haven't been aware of it."

"What is this, Al? Are you sore at me?"

"Hell no," he said, and he shrugged and smiled. "It was just an idle observation. So, okay, you have your little hunches."

"Well, I suppose we all go and read Shore now," she said.

"No, we read Kunitz."

"What do you mean?"

"All this here," and he tapped the newspaper. "It's all about Kunitz, don't you see? No one is talking about your friend Shore."

"*My* friend?"

"Your admirer."

"You're crazy, Al," she said and laughed. "Alright, so now we'll talk about Kunitz."

"You don't know anything about Kunitz."

"And you don't know anything about Shore."

"It's not going to worry me, you can bet on it," he said grimly. "Anyway, I told you, this kind of talk that'll be going around—you won't need to know anything about Shore. You finished your drink?"

39

"You want to go? Okay, let's go."

"I'll get the *New York Review* on the way out," he said.

Outside, the street was in a strange light. There were heavy, low, dark clouds overhead, but up at the head of the street, where the dominating insurance building stood, there was a patch of red sky shot through with blue. They crossed to Lisa's car in the parking lot.

On the way home he looked at the *Review* again and suddenly laughed. "Look, even *they* can't take Shore seriously. Levine hasn't done a drawing of Shore for the piece; he did Kunitz. They know the big attraction is Kunitz." At home, while Lisa was busy getting dinner, Al sat by the window, reading the Kunitz essay again. When he had finished, he lay back, struggling against his deepening professional embarrassment. The window was open. The curtain fluttered in a sudden cool breeze. It felt good on his head.

He was proud, stubborn. No one was going to tell him what he needed to read. He'd had enough of that stuff in graduate school. Sooner or later he might get around to Shore, but in his own good time; right now he had his own work to do.

"Come on, Al," Lisa called, and he sauntered into the dinner table, yawning lazily as he sat down, then rubbing his beard. "Kunitz did a pretty good piece there. Yes, you might want to take a look at it." Then he laughed. "In any event, it'll make Shore a nine days' wonder around here, even if nowhere else. Kunitz doesn't have the influence he used to have."

"What's that?" she asked, looking up from the plate she handed him. Catching something in his eyes, she said quickly: "Yes, of course," smiling with what seemed to him a superior, indulgent knowledge of his nature. It made him angry.

"This looks great," he said, taking the plate from her. "I don't know why you say you don't like to cook."

"I just hate cooking."

"I wouldn't mind being a great cook."

"I'm sure I'd eat everything you cooked."

But her condescending attitude toward him about Shore got under his skin. Two days later, in the middle of the afternoon, as he was sitting at his desk working, he felt so restless that he finally threw his pencil at the desk. He felt like doing something crazy—going to a Yonge Street massage parlor and having some naked girl flop her breasts over him or going to a horror movie. But he did not want to join his drinking friends at the Park Plaza. Then he thought of Lisa and asked himself what had made her feel she was entitled to have a superior, understanding knowledge of his nature. Lisa in a new light. . . . Something really new about her, which he didn't like at all; yet it could be explained. Maybe on the side, she had been secretly reading Shore since meeting him. Getting up, he wandered around the apartment, poking into corners and under pillows, then pulling out all the drawers in the dresser in the bedroom. He couldn't find a Shore book. Suddenly he stopped as if looking at himself in astonishment. "What the hell am I doing?" he said aloud. Why am I getting into this head-game with Lisa over this guy whom I hadn't the slightest interest in? Putting the whole thing out of his mind, he sat down and went back to work.

From that night on, he worked with fierce puritanical energy, letting nothing distract him, never giving in to the strange apathy that threatened him. He and Lisa did not mention Kunitz or Shore anymore. It was as if Lisa knew what attitude he wanted her to take.

Yet each day she looked more dreadfully prosaic to him in her blue jeans and sloppy sweater, the seat of her jeans always hanging loose. Soon he couldn't see anything but the baggy, hanging seat. "For God's sake, Lisa," he cried one night. "When we're here alone I'd like to see you in a dress sometime." Startled, she said, "Alright, Al. I thought there were other things—" and she went to the bedroom and put on a dress.

"Other things? What other things? What an excuse," he cried, following her. Then, hurt by her submissiveness, he

41

whispered: "No, no, Lisa." He told her to take off the dress. They went to bed, and he tried to take her warmly and completely in his arms, trying to hold on to her blindly as if he dared not believe that her novelty had worn away.

But the next day when she came home, he saw that she was exhausted. Her glow had faded. Stricken, he cried, "You can't work night and day. You're not to do any more housekeeping. I'll look after the house and do the cleaning while I'm planning my night's work."

"You can't do housework," she said angrily.

"Why not? Just think of me as unskilled labor."

He began to get up early in the morning and make her breakfast before she went to work. He had a hot meal ready when she came home at night. All this gave him a satisfaction he wouldn't admit, but it took him away from his work. He became very good with a mop and vacuum cleaner. Sometimes, while he swept and cleaned, he would come upon her, sitting on the bed, cutting and polishing her toenails, and he watched and waited, feeling lonely in his need for that lift she used to give him.

One night he caught Lisa watching him. "You look like a convict in that old locker-room sweater," she said. "I think it must be the sweater that's getting me down." And next night she came home with a beautiful, brown-and-black-striped sweater. When he had put it on, she frowned, then tears came to her eyes. "Lisa," he said. "In heaven's name, what's the matter?"

"I don't know. Maybe I had got used to you in the old sweater. How do I know? But I didn't notice."

"Notice what?"

"You look as worn-out as the day I picked you up. What's driving you, Al?"

"Nothing's driving me. I'm going good."

"Why isn't it good for *us*, Al? What's wrong with us? I don't seem to be here for you like I was. Nor you for me. Is it this town? Maybe the town isn't good for us now. The way you look at me sometimes? I feel . . . you're not even looking at me. It's like—" It was as if she wanted to say that in the beginning his too-searching glance had put a shadow between them, and now the shadow was deepening. "I mean, I think you need a holiday," she said impulsively. "Look. The bigger world outside, eh? You always wanted to look at the world. The big world. You always wanted to go to Europe."

"Sure."

"Let's get out of this town," she said. "The check will soon be here from father. Let's blow it on a couple of weeks in Europe." Her eagerness began to affect him. He felt himself whirling away from the town, from nameless things that were between them, and from a frame of mind that hit him every time he sat down at the desk. All they needed, he thought, was to run from town, then he would see her again in all her natural elegance, this time against the background of Paris or Rome. There the enchantment he knew was in her would touch him again. Laughing, he took her in his arms, whispering: "Lisa, Lisa, I remember telling old Mrs. Burnside that I would get to Europe, and now, it turns out, I only had to get to you."

In October the greens and golds of Rome had turned to brown. At twilight the dome of St. Peter's seemed bleak and cold, but in the daytime, there was splendid sunlight. They were at the hotel atop the Spanish Steps, and many movie people sat in the lounges on vast expanses of red carpet. One of these out-of-work directors, who had a bluff, warm, open air and gimlet eyes, speaking good colloquial English, said that Lisa had a head like the Egyptian queen, Nefertiti, but his eyes were on her legs. She wore a small brown leather miniskirt with a black crepe blouse and black stockings. Her long black hair and the black legs made your eyes go to the brown miniskirt.

The director suggested he could arrange a dinner with Alberto Moravia and some other intellectuals. Would Al like such a dinner? And while he was trying to con Al with his deliberate charm, his eyes were on Lisa's neck. "Well, let's have a drink and talk," Al said. When they were drinking, Al told him: "Drink up, my friend. Keep me company. What's the matter?" Al drank the director into a stupor, and they left him slumped in a chair. Al said grandly, "These Italians simply can't drink. Here in Rome, I can drink twice as much, eat twice as much, love twice as much."

44

"I didn't like that director, anyway," she said.

"He was full of malarkey; now he's full of booze."

"It wasn't the malarkey," she said. "It's that he dyes his hair."

"Before or after he pastes it on?"

"Al . . ." and she circled away, shaking with laughter—her own deep warming laughter.

He felt exuberant, full of himself and Lisa and Rome. After studying the street map, he decided to rent a car. They should have no traffic problems. Wasn't he an old taxi driver? In the little rented Ford Cortina they got hooked onto one-way streets heading for the Tiber. Cars honked at him; he honked and honked in reply, roaring with laughter. She giggled, she shrieked. Confused by the turnoffs, he always passed them. The one-way streets carried them out to the suburbs where they found some height of land so they could look back over the roofs and hills of Rome to the dome of St. Peter's. They used the dome as a marker as they made their way back. "It's alright," he said. "Who else has seen the suburbs of Rome? Lisa, no other woman in history has ever seen as much of Rome from so many different and distant angles as you have."

"With a born taxi driver, why not?" she said, giggling. "You know something, Al? A couple of weeks before we left I ran into one of your old girls—"

"Who?"

"What's it matter? Anyway, I asked her why she didn't hate you, and you know what she said? 'Oh, no, I like that man. He could make me laugh.'" And Lisa laughed. "Just the same, it's taken us all afternoon to cross the river. From now on, we're using a taxi." They used taxis and they went everywhere.

Al took it for granted that Lisa was also giving all her imagination to Rome, but sometimes there was a surprised, lost look on her face. She said she liked the new Rome, the living people, the Via Condotti and the Corso. Al had a remarkable textbook knowledge of the ancient city and the ancient figures, and now that he was on their ground, they came alive for him. They were with him wherever he went. He bawled them out, belittled them, saw right through them. Standing before the

45

Pantheon with Lisa he said: "Hadrian, now there was a superior man. There's a guy I could have got along with." The night they climbed the great floodlit steps to the Campidoglio, he stood breathless and wondering in the square, feeling in Michelangelo's architecture another intimation of order and harmony. Then confronting Marcus Aurelius up there on his horse, he suddenly grabbed Lisa and danced her around the statue till she stumbled on the cobblestones, and he, out of breath, looked up at the emperor and cried: "Here we are, old Marcus. What do you think?"

"To hell with what he thinks," she said.

"Come on, Lisa."

"Oh, Al, come on yourself."

"I like that horse."

"Every kid goes for a big tin horse," she said, sounding bored as she sauntered away.

Catching up with her, he complained: "It's the biggest damned horse you ever saw." He had her arm and felt her shoulder go up stiffly. Then he knew that she felt neglected, and he trembled with resentment. Rome was the loveliest of all the cities, and here she was, wanting to be treated as the only really lovely thing in Rome. From then on, he was aware of other surprising little oppositions. He liked wandering at loose ends: unexpected ruins, restaurants, boutiques, tie shops and churches—they all delighted him. Then, if he suddenly wanted to cross the road, she argued; it wasn't where they had planned to cross. In Christ's name, what does it matter? and he was harsh with her, for there seemed to be a map in her head which only she knew and he couldn't know; if they didn't follow her secret map, everything would go to pieces.

They set aside a morning for St. Peter's, and it rained. They waited until late afternoon, then the sun came out and they agreed to spend an hour at St. Peter's and afterwards go to the cafe on the Piazza del Popolo. She liked this cafe. The young women and men looked as young people were supposed to look in Rome, she said. When they entered St. Peter's, he whispered, "My God, it's the treasure house of the last 500 years of

Europe." Wandering around, he told her he loved the burnt siennas and grays of the marbles. Near the Pope's high altar, with its twisting Bernini columns, he said: "It's a funny thing, Lisa. Here I'm not awed by God but by the genius of man."

"Al, it's been an hour." She was tugging at his sleeve. "Let's go."

"An hour. What the hell?"

"You said an hour."

"Lisa, in St. Peter's I'm not punching a clock."

"Okay."

"Wait. Where are you going?"

"Outside. I'll wait for you."

He watched her go down the center aisle, a yellow hand-kerchief around her head, a small figure in the vast basilica, the click of her heels very hard. He followed her. At the door he grabbed her by the arm. Pilgrims stared as they stepped outside. He said: "I may never have a chance to see this place again."

"Go to it," she said, "I'll be here on the steps."

"No, you won't. That guy over there won't let you." A middle-aged functionary had the job of shooing away any girls sitting on the great flight of steps. He shooed them like pigeons, watching them flutter away. "He won't bother me," she said disdainfully.

"It's time someone bothered you. All this bickering, all about a lot of garbage." Then, concerned, suddenly gentle, he said: "Look, has something happened?"

"To me?"

"Are you pregnant?"

"Are you crazy?"

"Lisa, you're not yourself."

"Who am I, then?"

"Who do you think you are?"

"Helen of Troy, you dumdum." As his hand went out to her, she knocked it away fiercely. She came closer, stiffening, her head back, angry and a darkness in her face, and he felt a tearing at him, desperate, silent. She was trying to snatch back

47

something of herself and hide it from him in her darkness. He stood gaping at her. As he showed his surprise, her face was full of wild satisfaction. She sauntered away and sat down on a lower step, staring across the vast cobblestone square at the colonnade, indifferent to the approach of the custodian of the steps.

"All right, damn it," he called. "Stay there," and he went back into the church. He wandered around, thinking she might come in. After all, she was the Catholic. No, his little convent girl was sitting out there on the steps, waiting to be shooed away. He found he couldn't concentrate, and left. She was half-way down, the only one on the vast steps. The old functionary far over on the left paid no attention to her.

"Lisa," he said awkwardly, "I might as well have stayed with you. I was out here with you all the time." "Al," she said and jumped up and kissed him. There was a taxi stand at the gate. They went to "her" cafe on the Corso. It was getting dark, so she couldn't look up at the Pincio. They went to Alfredo's in Trastevere where a musician and a singer hovered around their table, making up flattering songs. Then they went back to the hotel and were tender with each other. They wondered why they kept bickering. They lay on the bed and made love.

It was not yet midnight. He could hear the noise from the Via Veneto, horns honking and motorcycle engines roaring. He began to dress. Sitting up, she watched him. "Okay," she said lazily, reaching for her stockings. Her long black hair fell over her breasts as she crossed a leg, and her head rose as she drew the stocking high up on her thigh, sticking her leg out at him impishly in lazy satisfaction. He looked idly, then again more alertly. Something bothered him. Something suddenly was shatteringly wrong. The roguish gesture with her leg and her smile: it was familiar, expected. They were now just another man and woman in a hotel room, who after a day of bickering, made love and felt a little better. All open to each other, Lisa now all open to him. Her shadows were all gone and with her shadows, the secret places.

"Let's go over to the Via Veneto," he said, shaken, and turning away quickly.

"Fine."

"Hurry."

They sat on the glassed-in, pink-awninged terrace at the Cafe de Paris, watching worldly international faces. The Italian girls wore sweater coats with superb style, Lisa said. She would buy one for herself. A gray-haired man, sitting alone beside them, listening and glancing at Lisa, suddenly said with a courtly ease, "Excuse me. We speak the same language, so let me introduce myself. Marcus Stevens."

"Marcus Stevens?" Al said, "Well, my goodness." The well-known American poet and scholar was an established figure in the academic world. "This is great," Al said, shaking hands. Stevens bought them a drink. "Where are you from?" Stevens asked, being very courtly with Lisa. When she told him, he said, "Ah, really? Doesn't Eugene Shore live there?"

"I see you've read that Kunitz article," Al said, smiling cynically. He had a sudden resentful feeling that Shore was some ghost after him, on his trail.

"Kunitz? Seems to me he's got to Shore a little late."

"Well, at least everybody in our town knows about Shore now."

"I dare say," Stevens agreed and began to talk about a quality he thought remarkable in the Shore books. The talk became an exciting lecture until Al, attempting a sympathetic insight, found Stevens lifting his left eyebrow at him. Then he blushed. "Anyway," Stevens continued, "when you get back home and run into Shore, tell him how much I admire his work, will you?" They shook hands, and Stevens left.

Brooding, Al glanced at Lisa who held his eyes. "He saw that you don't know a damn thing about Shore, Al." He saw that she was trying hard not to laugh at him. Scowling, he held himself in, afraid he was going to lash out at her. "It's not funny, Lisa. I have to respect my own world. Sooner or later I know that guy'll come into my stamping ground. Oh, hell." He called the waiter. Then, walking along the street, he stopped suddenly by a kiosk with a lavish display of paperbacks under a brilliant light. Across the street, at the entrance to the Excelsior Hotel, stood an exuberant group, probably Americans.

"Forget him, Al," Lisa said, taking his arm.

"To hell with that man. I feel restless. That's all."

"Anything I can do for you, Mr. Delaney?"

"Yeah. Stop upsetting me."

"That's all I've done here, isn't it, Al?" she said quietly.

"Here? You don't like it here?"

"Not any more. No." Her head was at that proud, superior angle, but her lips quivered. Her eyes shifted as if she didn't care where she was. It was as if she had known his thoughts in the hotel room, and her insight frightened him. Something was lost, something ended—and she knew.

"It's alright," he said, taking her arm almost shyly. "It's Paris tomorrow, isn't it?" But he couldn't bear his emptiness, so much like the painful loneliness he had felt during his oral defense, when he had heard the voice whispering, "You're nothing, Al."

They left for Paris in the late afternoon and took a room at the Intercontinental Hotel on the Rue de Rivoli. Al would have preferred the Left Bank. No, Lisa said, they should feel opulent. It would do him good, both here and back home, and they could go over to the Left Bank every day. Paris was chilly under the fitful sunlight, and the horse chestnut trees were bare. The wild stimulation Al had expected and dreamed of in this city was blunted as soon as he entered the lobby of the ornate old palace hotel. Holding her arm, he again felt lonely, and the loneliness was in the touch of his own hand. It was the same when they were in the bedroom. But that night, when he tried staying down in the lobby by himself, then standing at the door watching the prostitutes in their little cars bringing their customers back to the hotel, he was dismayed to think of Lisa in the bedroom by herself, and he went up to her. With all his heart he wanted her to be happy in Paris, not have one cross word with him, to go only to the places she wanted to go to. He wanted her to feel she was all of Paris to him.

They had told Jake Fulton they would visit all the Scott Fitzgerald cafes and bars. They had become so real for Jake since he had worked on his thesis. Al wrote Jake that the

Coupole and the Select were still there, but the Coupole, fashionable now, had been reclaimed by the French, while the La Closerie des Lilas was very expensive, even for Lisa. They sat, in turn, at these three famous cafes. In one they played pool, and his mind being on other things, Al let Lisa beat him. "Good God! Imagine! I'm the champ," she cried. With a wild laugh she fled from the cafe. "Come on, another game, Lisa," he called, catching up to her.

"Oh no you don't," she was laughing, and as they wandered along Montparnasse he tried to coax her, but she said solemnly: "I like being the champ." They laughed and pushed and pulled at each other, and later in the evening, sitting at the Falstaff bar, she said: "You know something, Al? I'm retiring undefeated," and she smiled graciously. "You're the champ again." They had a drink on it.

The Falstaff was a cozy, paneled dining room and bar in the old English style. The bar was of heavy, shining, golden oak. On the stool beside Al was a thin, hawk-nosed, blue-eyed man, redhaired and heavy-browed, who wore a tweed jacket with leather on the elbows. He talked to the bartender in English. The dapper little bartender spoke excellent English with a slight cockney accent that suggested he had spent some years in London. Together they gossiped about the London theater.

"That was a good piece you wrote about Sam in the *New Statesman*," the bartender said. "Well, Beckett will surely be in tomorrow night."

Samuel Beckett, Al thought, quickening. It was incredible. Another literary bartender. What went on among bartenders these days? Still, in the books about the Paris of 40 years ago, they all spoke of a bartender at the Falstaff called Jimmy. All the writers had talked to Jimmy about their work. Did a man applying for a job as barkeep at the Falstaff have to pass a required-reading test? When the bartender moved off for a moment, Al said to the hawk-nosed man: "Excuse me, I overheard you talking about Beckett." Al introduced himself and Lisa. The man was a Welsh poet named Evans.

51

"It must be great to know Beckett," Al said.

"Well, anybody can know about Beckett now," Evans said. "I knew him when hardly anyone else did."

"That's the real thing," Al said. "Ever hear of Eugene Shore?"

"Who?"

"Shore."

"Never heard of him."

"Well, if you're for Beckett, you'd certainly like Shore," Al said. He started talking about Shore with a quiet, persuasive enthusiasm, offering all the insights Marcus Stevens had given him in Rome. Almost word for word, he offered them, fascinated by the Welshman's growing interest. The bartender also listened respectfully. Finally the Welshman said: "I'm sorry I have to go. I really do." Evans bought the bartender a drink, bowed to Lisa, and left, leaving Al, his head in his hands over the bar, hating himself.

"Just what got into you, Mr. Delaney?" Lisa asked, calmly.

"Oh, please, please shut up," he whispered.

"Oh, come on, Al."

He stared morosely at the shining oak.

"Look," she said casually, "why not be a pro? When we get home, look up Shore."

"Lisa, the old pro. The researcher."

"Certainly. I'm damn good at it. Look up Shore. I'll go with you."

"Don't you think we might read a book of his first? Or do you TV pros ever have to read a book? Come on." They left abruptly. On Montparnasse she stopped, aloof and by herself, elegant in her yellow pants suit, staring across the road at the Select. With a beautiful sadness in her face, she said, her voice breaking, "You know something, Al. I don't think Paris is going to live forever in my heart. It'll be better when we get home and you're working. I know it will," and she took his arm.

The day before they left Paris, while Lisa shopped on Rue

Honore, he found an English bookshop and, to his surprise, one of Shore's novels. On the plane there were many empty seats. While Lisa slept, Al began reading. Shore's style was unadorned and colloquial. It could even be called common-place, he thought with the same savage pleasure he might have taken marking the paper of a hostile student. His pencil in hand, he marked phrases that should have been made more striking. At about the tenth page he snorted: "Oh, this will never do, never. His verbs are all weak." Then the ease of the style and the story began to hold him. Without noticing, he had put his pencil back in his breast pocket. Waking, Lisa called the steward for a gin and tonic. When she drank she stared straight ahead and then at Al, and when she was finished she put her head back and, before dozing again, murmured: "Must be inter-esting."

"Yeah," he said quietly, off by himself, far away from her. He went on reading the story about the dangerous criminal, a bank robber who had been paroled. His reappearance in the town had dazzled the citizens: the big-time thief had believed in their goodwill. Carried away, charmed by himself and his own way of seeing the situation, he had tried to set himself up as a lifeline of hope for all condemned men and ex-cons, while the town waited expectantly for him to commit some terrible act of violence. This is very peculiar, Al thought. Quickly he turned back to the title page for the publication date. Then he felt that curious, secret, almost excited, warmth of discovery. Closing his eyes, he saw himself telling his colleagues: "The criminal saint. It's incredible, but there it is. Twenty years before Genêt! Yet, it's not the saint of Genêt and Sartre. In fact"—and now he was talking to himself, pleased, staring out the little window of the plane—"I've never been sure that Sartre understands saints. For all the bigness of his book, I don't think he understands criminals. Suppose you had two or three Genêts. So much for the saintly, singular view."

In his excitement Al wanted to make many notes because these were the kind of free-wheeling thoughts that would slip

53

away. Then he sighed and rubbed his beard. He didn't have his journal with him. He had to make do with a few marginal notes on the back of the title page. He read on.

When he was finished, he lay back, stirred by his understanding of the great and shabby grandeur of Shore's ex-con, released, put on parade, and then shot down, the man of charm and compassion, so condemned. And the girl in the book. The big, wild fellow had groped his way toward her, half knowing that she might give his life another meaning. What a strange effect, Al thought. The plane was sailing over a white floor of clouds rolled together like snowdrifts in endless, Arctic space.

Lisa coughed, moving restlessly, and he looked at her. Her long hair was askew, a drop of perspiration on her upper lip, her rumpled dress well above her knees. As she wet her lips with her tongue, her hand came out, touching him while his mind was filled with the characters from Shore's story. The touch brought her alive among those characters, and in that moment, held in the story's knowing compassionate light, she too appeared to be movingly new, yet just herself, and in this vision he was reaching for her. In the sky, a small sea of blue broke through the snowy wasteland—a cold, brilliant, icy sea in sunlight.

7

Saying nothing to Lisa after coming home, Al tried to reach Shore. He wrote him, then telephoned him; no answer. He knew no one in the academic world who had any connection with Shore, nor anyone else in town, who could help him. Finally in the second week in November, in an unseasonable snowstorm, when he was downtown, coming out of a department store, he made up his mind. He knew what he was going to do. It was late in the afternoon. The street lights had come on. The heavily falling snow was easy to take because the air was so mild. Stopping to turn up his coat collar, he watched some women with umbrellas coming down the street. They had the umbrellas because they had thought it was going to rain. Heavy with snow, the umbrellas looked like white flowers drifting along under the street lights. Right then Al knew that he was only doing what he had to do.

He went hurrying through the snow, going east two blocks, then up Bond Street to the publishing house. He told the girl at the switchboard that he was a friend of Dr. Morton Hyland, who had advised him to see the editor. He liked the lie because it immediately got him into the editor's office. The editor, a slight, bald man with glasses, asked about Dr. Hyland's health.

They agreed that the professor should be taking better care of himself. Then Al told him about his idea for a short, critical book about Eugene Shore. "Who is the man who writes these books?" Al said. "That was Kunitz' big question. It was everybody's question."

Al didn't mention that he'd already been rebuffed by Shore. Shore was the coming man, he went on; he would get bigger and bigger. The 12 Shore books were at his fingertips. His own book on Shore would be the first one, the source, and inevitably, it would be required reading in colleges. The editor, who had read the Kunitz article, became enthusiastic. He offered Al a contract and a small advance and asked to be remembered to Dr. Hyland.

As Al went out, he thought excitedly: "I'll have a go at it. Maybe it'll pay off. Get it done quick and then move on to Mailer. Two birds in the bush. . . ."

In the hall, taking off his coat, he listened and heard Lisa moving around in the kitchen. Half apprehensive, half grim, he sauntered along the hall.

"Is it still snowing?" she asked.

"It sure is. It's really coming down now."

"It's crazy," she said. "Only the second week in November, and heavy snow."

"It'll turn to rain and be all gone by tomorrow. It's mild out."

"I just got in myself," she said. "I was having a cup of coffee before I get dinner. Want one?"

"Sure," he said, sitting down at the end of the kitchen table. When she too had sat down and was sipping her coffee, he said: "Listen, Lisa. I've been busy. I've been to see a publisher. A big change in my plans." While he told her what he had done, he watched her face.

"I see. Why didn't you tell me about this?"

"Well, there was the Mailer thing. I thought you might think I should go on with it."

"Do I give a damn about Mailer?"

"I don't know," he said. In the sudden silence her face was full of surprise and wonder. He couldn't believe she wasn't going to protest against him wasting so much time at her expense, and he tightened up, ready to struggle with her.

"It's an odd thing," she said softly. "Yes, a very odd thing," she repeated, half to herself. Her remote, wandering smile hurt him. "It's like . . . it's as if Shore kept after you, and you couldn't shake him off and—"

"And what?"

"Well," she began, still bemused, "I suppose it was a case of, why go to Italy?"

"So we went to Italy."

"Come on, scholar. You know those lines."

"No, I don't."

" 'Why go to Italy who cannot circumnavigate the sea of thoughts and things at home?' My wandering father used to feed me that."

"You must have found that funny."

"Al, maybe this is a coming home."

"Coming home?"

"To our own world."

"For God's sake, you make this sound like a beer commercial."

"I *did* get that feeling, right at the first, with Shore."

"Oh, Jesus," he said, his voice breaking angrily. "You think you have some line on Shore because he gave you a look. This'll take up most of my life now, don't you understand, just trying to get hold of him?" He jumped up, his arm swinging as he went closer. He'd knocked the cup from her hand, and it shattered on the floor. As coffee spilled over the table, dripping on her housecoat, she too stood up, shocked, her face full of changing surprise.

Facing him, with the coffee on the table coming in a slow stream toward him, she said: "What in hell is this, Al? Everything's okay." She laughed and got a dishrag and cleaned the table. When she sat down again, she was still smiling. She told

57

him she could do his research for him and help him with his typing, too. Then she said, "What do you do now? Get in touch with Shore?"

"Oh, don't go into that, Lisa. I've written to him twice."

"What'd he say?"

"A stupid formal card: Mr. Shore doesn't see scholars."

"How about phoning him?"

"I've called him twice."

"What did he say?"

"I can't get to him. They said he doesn't give interviews."

"I see." Her chin in her hand and elbow on the table, she was lost in thought. "Isn't it maddening?" she said finally. "There he is, only a couple of miles away from us."

"I'll tell you who I can call," he said, standing up.

"Who?"

"Starkey Kunitz."

"In New York?"

"He should be in the New York phone book if he lives there. I'll get the operator to get his number. This could be a good time right now," he said. "Anyway, what's to lose?"

"Boy," she said, "you've got more nerve than Dick Tracy," following him to the phone. "Why not?" he said. "I'll tell him I'm writing the first book on Shore because of him. Lisa, he's got to be interested." She sat down beside him so she could listen too. When the operator got the Kunitz number, they waited, looking at each other through the ringing. When Kunitz himself answered, Al could hardly speak he was so surprised.

"Al Delaney, Mr. Kunitz," he said. "It's all right," he added quickly, "I understand why you don't talk to scholars. But in your article on Shore you spoke of certain effects. Believe me, Mr. Kunitz, that's the thing," he blurted out. "If I'm to go on with my book, I have to believe there's someone else in the world, who—"

Kunitz had a crisp, gruff voice, like an old British colonel. "Oh, for God's sake," he began impatiently. There was a silence. Al thought he had hung up. Then Kunitz said quietly: "You are quite right, Mr. Delaney. On certain pages in those

Shore books there are very definite effects. I'm an old hand at telling how these things are achieved. I went over and over those pages. Damned if I know how it's done. If you must know, it took me longer to write that Shore piece than any piece I've written in years. What looks ordinary on the surface is really extraordinary. Good luck to you." And he hung up.

"Well, well, well," Al said softly as he got up from the telephone chair. "I sure am going to have one reader."

"Kunitz?"

"The great Kunitz."

"You feel good, don't you?"

"I sure do."

"So do I," she said, but then she began to walk up and down restlessly, going back and forth to the window. Finally she stood there looking out. "That snow in the street light—the way it falls. I used to love it when I was a child." Turning to him quickly she said, "Let's eat out. Let's go to some Chinese place and go on from there? What do you say? Do I look alright in this?"

"Just get your coat," he said.

They had dinner at the Sai Woo, then went on to the Macambo bar to make a night of it. The lounge was crowded with young people, but the loud blues band, and even the happy faces around them, intruded on their good silent moments. "Let's go; let's walk," Al said restlessly.

Outside, it had stopped snowing, but there were four inches of snow on the sidewalks. Down the street a taxi stuck at the curb was spinning its wheels wildly.

"Everything looks so peaceful on such a night," Lisa said. They agreed that the city at night after a snowfall was always lovely. Old, battered houses, stores, and chimneys blended in the night's soft glow that had its own winter warmth for the eye. It started to snow again. The flakes falling on Lisa's head and shoulders put her face in a white mantle behind the veil of falling snow. In that light her face enchanted Al, and she knew it. They trudged along in drifts that came over the tops of their boots. The ease in their silence held its own secret. Suddenly,

59

Lisa said: "Have you thought of this, Al? Our Eugene Shore, he may be the first great one named Shore."

"Oh, I don't know," he said. "There's that other fine family, The Distant Shores."

And she said gravely: "Yes, and there was the big hockey player, Eddie Shore." "Right," he agreed, trying not to laugh, "and there's Toots Shore." "Don't forget Dinah Shore," she said. "No, I like pull for the Shore. Pullford Shore." Just then, her foot slipped into a snow bank, and he cried: "What is this, Lisa? We're fools. You're going to catch pneumonia. Come on. Let's go home."

But of course they couldn't get a taxi. They had another half hour's walk. When they finally got home Lisa had a drink of hot whiskey and went to bed, but Al after changing his clothes, worked on the outline for the book.

8

Still going his own way, safe in his polite neighborhood, still taking his walk downtown, Eugene Shore might have thought he could go on keeping people like Al Delaney out of his private life. But Al, for his part, sticking to his room just a few minutes away, had a little game he played that got him right to Shore. With a little concentration he seemed to see Shore, see him in the rocking chair as he had seen him through the window. Then he could imagine he was tearing the stuff he wanted out of him. He had the tools. He sought out the themes, archetypal figures, traces of old myths, and interesting ambiguities. Sometimes he would pause, hearing Lisa shuffling along the hall in the comfortable pair of old slippers she wore. The flopping sound of the slippers would end outside his room, and in the sudden silence while she listened, he felt all her approval. He felt it, too, when she told him she liked falling asleep listening to the sound of the typewriter. But also when, around midnight, she would come into the room and say, "How about taking a break? How about a cup of coffee and a sandwich or a cold beer?" She was taking the stuff he was writing to work and typing it. Soon he had 120 pages.

One night when there was a heavy cold rain, Al began to reread the pages. He read through the cracks of thunder and lightning flashes and the sound of rain splashing against the window. He didn't even look up. Suddenly he knew he wasn't reading; he was too shaken. Something was terribly wrong. Nothing in these pages said anything about the effect Shore's work had had on him. "Oh, my God," he said.

He got up and wandered out into the kitchen. He was glad Lisa was asleep. He wanted to rush out and get drunk in some bar, but the hour was too late and the rain too heavy. He got a can of beer out of the refrigerator. While he drank it, a heaviness like the touch of some kind of death in him began to frighten him. Then he hated himself for what he was. Again he heard that old voice: "You're nothing, Al." Just another scholarly little hack. No, not just another one, he thought in a desperate gesture to himself. At least he could see that he was hacking it. At least he could see how he had been trapped by all his scholarly training and how, no matter where he roamed now, he would have his albatross—Dr. Morton Hyland—perched on his neck the rest of his life. The tool case. Goddamned tools that didn't work.

Even the beer. Looking at the glass and the empty cans, he felt sorry for himself. He rarely drank beer. Whiskey or brandy! Scotch or rye! Why was there no whiskey in the house? Then he held his head, growing more frightened. He knew he was going to quit on Shore. He would have to have the guts to suffer the humiliation and go back to finishing up with Mailer. He said this to himself over and over again while he stared at the shiny, white-enameled table.

Suddenly he jumped up and went lurching along the hall to his desk. He got out all the old clippings Lisa had brought him and began to go through them, fumbling eagerly, as if he remembered vaguely that these interesting comments from some remarkable men had told him something he should have kept in mind. Yet why were the comments so brief? Sinclair Lewis, years ago when Shore was young: "Shore's technique is so simple he seems to have none at all"; and Wyndham Lewis and William Saroyan and Alfred Kazin. Ancient, admiring comments, as if these men, too, had touched on something they couldn't figure out and had hurried away. What was Shore? A Christian? A pagan? An atheist? Even Kunitz had mentioned an "effect," a strange, general effect. Something Kunitz himself couldn't figure out, and he had been too smart to try. A magic cement. That's it. That's it. Magic! Al thought. Then he leaned back in the chair, nursing a sense of relief he didn't understand, an almost joyous release.

Suddenly he stood up, frowning. He remembered something that made him feel awkward, then painfully embarrassed. Finally he went to the drawer and took out his journal, opening it at the page he had labeled *Lisa*. That page, thank God, was still blank. At least on that page, in spite of himself, he had let something be. Let Lisa be. In spite of that night in Rome, when he had looked at her, thinking something was finished, he had had to let her be. He ripped the page from the journal. Crumpling it in his hand he tossed it at the basket and then went hesitantly into the bedroom.

"Lisa, Lisa," he said, shaking her gently. In the gray light from the window, his face looked strained. She was startled.

"What is it, Al? What happened?"

"I just had to tell you something," he said. Sitting on the side of the bed, talking softly, he now had that mixture of energy and elation she found irresistible.

"You know how I've always been driven to try and understand everything. I somehow seem to know in my gut now that there are beautiful things that can't be explained. I don't think they can be—"

While listening, she caressed the back of his neck, soothing him. Then she drew him down. His inner excitement always seemed to stimulate her sexually. She said nothing until the next night at 8:30 when she came into his room full of curiosity. "What's been going on here?" she asked, sitting down on his couch. Her legs were crossed, her straight hair masked one side of her face. Deeply moved, he couldn't take his eyes off her. "Lisa. This is the whole thing. What is it that makes you Lisa?" he asked softly. "Your thighs are a little lean. . . ."

"What?"

"About eight inches above the knee there."

"Sorry about that."

"Your mouth, your neck. It still isn't you."

"Isn't it?"

"No. Maybe it's magic."

Then her wondering stillness pulled him to her. As he bent over her, she drew him down and undid his shirt, kissing him gently again and again until he was beside her. It was the first time they had made love on this couch. It had been a part of his working space. Afterward, lying at ease with their hands linked, he said: "Soon we'll have made love all over the house."

"Take the night off, Al. Let's go someplace."

"I'd like to go to the circus," he said.

"Why the circus?"

"See clowns on stilts 40 feet high."

"I see them every day," she said.

"I see them every night," he said. "Yeah, so I do," he repeated, struck by the fancy, then held, staring at her, his smile vanishing as a little voice within him whispered, "Not just clowns, criminals on stilts 40 feet high." Then, still staring at her raptly, he remembered how stirred he had been by Shore's big, poetic bank robber, and how he had seen himself and Lisa drawn into the moving warmth of the big criminal's aura. The big sincere one! The town's clown for a day. In every Shore book, he could see now, there was some kind of endearing clown-criminal, a stubborn young priest who had to be confined. A wilful young girl on her own white horse. A whole company of strange clown-outlaws in the circus of life.

So absorbed was he in his thoughts that he didn't notice that Lisa had quietly left him there alone. When he finally looked around, he knew he couldn't remain cooped up there. He felt too restless, his imagination too unsatisfied. He grabbed his jacket and raincoat and hurried out.

At that hour the street was deserted. An ambulance, its red

light flashing around him as it passed, filled the street with fire, then with deeper darkness after it had gone. He went by unlighted houses and darkened apartment buildings. Farther downtown were the office spires whose lights were fading in the first thin morning light. Al didn't care where he was going. He was absorbed in what he thought was his first real glimpse of a unity he was sure existed in Shore's work. What was it? Not the burglar or ruthless apes or stock market thieves or lying politicians. Spiritual riff-raff. No, Shore's kind of criminals— they were like lovers knowing only the law of their own love, their actions surely rooted in a common criminality whether they were boundless lovers like that priest who had to be caught by the little cops of his own tribe and put away, or the bank robbers.

But I've only known about the cheap criminal mind, Al thought. In his taxi-driving days he had encountered hundreds of little guys, popcorn pimps, thugs, shit-heel thieves, all on the run, sprawling around in his taxi, bragging, bringing up from fright, and he had driven them to their hangouts and hide-outs. This was the ugly, stimulating world that had kept him sane through graduate school. But these taxicab criminals! Just pale pasteups of the Mr. Big they all believed ran everything.

High towers shone suddenly in the early light. The street he was in now was a great dark gully, yet he felt he was up there in the light, big with his own power, big with imagination, while down in the dark gullies, on their stilts 40 feet high, came all Shore's great clowns, walking stiffly, clumsily, their heads in the light, but their great stilts knocking aside the little gray men in the shadowed streets. Suddenly exalted, Al found himself walking among them in a town full of men with offices richly clean, their knives and guns registered with their cops, their words registered too, but he himself was up there with the ones on stilts, clumsy, high and in the open. Finally he turned home. When he got there and into his room without waking Lisa, he sat up, scribbling his notes. This is what he should do every night, he thought. The exhilarating walk, the work at home. Soon he had a sheaf of these "insights," as he called them. When he was out, Lisa would type up the pages, and when he came home he would go happily through the stack of new pages, exulting in the way the work was going.

One night just before 3:00 A.M. Al returned home and saw that
there was a light in his room. The light startled him, because he
remembered turning it out, so he hurried along the hall. Lisa
was there, her arms folded on the typewriter, her head buried
in them. "Lisa, Lisa, what in the world is the matter?"

"Just don't know what to say," she began and then faltered.
"I've been reading this stuff—" Then she tried to sound light
and casual. "Well, I don't know. I guess the world is full of all
kinds of criminals, and some are really grandly human enough
to be clowns or saints. I don't know. I always thought the world
was full of cops."

"Sure it is."

"All right," she tried to joke, "where is the cop?"

"What cop?"

"Shouldn't there be a cop. I mean—"

"Cut it out, Lisa."

"Well, what can I say?" she asked, meeting his eyes and
faltering again. Then utterly dismayed, she blurted out: "I've
gone over all this new stuff getting it together. When I was
typing I noticed it was all bits and pieces. Nothing coming
together. I thought you were writing a book. Goddamn it, I can't

focus on anything now. No one could get this stuff together. Al, it's not like you." Then her voice broke. Her head went back fiercely, she was so moved. "This stuff—great clowns and criminals and lovers—why are you so fearfully uncertain about them and everything else? These, these uncertain, random impressions! Why can't you be like you were in Rome? I know I wasn't so enthusiastic then, but now I see something. In Rome your mind was wonderfully full of those wild antique criminal figures, those ghosts—those great antique emperors and clowns and lovers, all so alive in your mind—the old Roman circus, and you were the ringmaster. You could laugh about them. My God, Al, you made me feel you could be one of them."

"Lisa, this isn't Rome," he said gently. He wasn't hurt, but his easy laugh made her jump up, facing him in her housecoat, her mouth trembling. He saw that she felt betrayed by her weeks of elation. Then the pain in her eyes really hurt him, and he shook his head. He wanted to be gentle and all open to her. "Lisa, you shouldn't do this, you know," he said, smiling as he put his arms around her. "You shouldn't make up your mind about the look of a thing that's all in pieces. Lisa, come on. Sit down." Drawing her down to the couch, lying back on the pillows stacked against the wall, he began to talk to her. "Don't patronize me, Al," she said, stiffening. "No, no, just try and understand," he said and kept running his fingers through her hair as he talked. "What you don't see, Lisa," he said, "is that I could get this whole thing together in a night or two if I wanted to. Just one or two things—things about Shore himself—and it all comes together." His hand falling to her shoulder, his arm tightening around her, gradually made her feel his intellectual delight in what he was doing. He did what he always could do when he was carried away—he enchanted her. "I have a feeling there are vistas opening up, Lisa. Vistas I must not exhaust," he whispered. "I mustn't close the book on them. There are things I know I must respond to even if I'm not certain of my responses. I only know I must not lose this while trying to finish Shore off."

When he talked like this, he filled her with strange expectations. But when he finally fell silent, she suddenly sat up.

68

"Al, if you don't get finished, what about your Mailer book? What about your job?"

"I haven't been thinking about it."

"But I thought—" She shook her head in bewilderment and began to pace up and down. Finally she turned to him gently: "Al, will you listen to me?"

"Of course I will."

"Maybe all this stuff *could* be great if it could only come together," she said carefully. "Maybe if you could just look at Shore with your own eyes—" Then her voice broke. "You can look at me so searchingly, Al, as no one else ever looked at me, and I love it, and you don't know how much I want it to go on. Well, if you could look at Shore just as searchingly, all this stuff might come together, and you'd be so excited about getting the thing down and seeing it finished. Al, will you see Shore?"

"Will I see Shore?" He sat up slowly. "Are you crazy, Lisa? You know I'd love to see him. *He* won't see *me.*"

"Do you mind if I see him?"

"You! How are *you* going to see him?"

"I don't know. Just walk in on him, I guess."

"Lisa, no one walks in on Shore."

"Well, I just feel in my bones that I could get away with it."

"Lisa," he began and wanted to laugh. But as she faced him so calm and full of herself, she had such dignity that he couldn't laugh. "You're quite a girl, but I don't think I'll see you come walking in here with Mr. Shore." With a shrug she walked out, and he sat there wondering and listening to her moving quickly around in the bedroom.

10

Lisa parked her car just down the street from Shore's house at 8:30 in the evening, when lights were on in all the houses. She went to the door, but the housekeeper said Mr. Shore was across the bridge getting some tobacco at the little store and should be back in a few minutes. The housekeeper hadn't asked her to come in and wait, so she was now walking slowly up and down in front of the house, with it starting to drizzle, half snow and half rain. The piled-up, dead leaves had whitening snow caps in the passing car lights. Shivering a little in her severe, elegantly cut black coat with the red silk scarf over her hair, she wished she had worn her rubbers. Then she saw Shore coming toward her. She let him get close, then called softly: "Mr. Shore?"

"Yes?"

"Remember me?"

"Ah, yes, indeed, I do."

"I thought you might. My name is Lisa Tolen."

"Lisa? Well, what's this about, Lisa?"

"Al Delaney."

"Who's he?"

"He was with me the night I came here."

71

"Ah, that's right. There was someone behind you."

"He's kept after you, asking you to see him. Why won't you see him, Mr. Shore?"

"That one, eh? Well, now, Lisa," he began, trying to laugh. "A man like me can't see scholars who are just doing their jobs. It's an industry. It's like industrial work," and he shrugged.

"I don't know anything about that kind of thing," and her head went back, then going closer to him she touched his arm. "Look at me," she said calmly. "Al is my whole life."

"Your whole life?" and he did look at her, then nodded and nodded again. "Lisa's life," he said gently. It was all he said, as he took her arm, walking her along with him. She didn't know where they were going. It didn't matter. She relaxed in the warm feeling of being at ease. Now she could be freely herself, only more warmly enlarged and appreciated. "I'm visiting some friends a few blocks away," he said. "It's my night to play poker. I'm late. As we walk along, you tell me about your Al Delaney."

Talking quickly and easily she told him she was living with Al, supporting him, and how Al had been working on Mailer and having no trouble, and how suddenly he had quit and turned to him.

"Just a minute," he said. "What's wrong with Mailer?"

"I think Al just got tired of him."

"Hmmm."

"Now he's got some wild view of you. He has a university appointment coming up if he finishes. I think he's in love with . . . this is crazy, I know . . . in love with *not* finishing. It frightens me that he doesn't want to be finished. Is he a little mad?"

"I never drove anyone mad, Lisa. I'm really a tame pussycat."

They had walked up from his ravine street and turned west. Now they were at a traffic intersection where three streets at different angles converged to this point on the main thoroughfare. Cars came from five directions into the one gleaming black hub of an intersection, the headlights swinging over the whitened lawns as the cars turned. "What do you think we should do, Lisa?" he asked.

"I think things might come together for him if you talked to him," she said. "Then he'd really want to finish. How about seeing him?"

"Well, now—"

"Please, Mr. Shore." She smiled.

"I've been a very private person, Lisa," he said uneasily, though held by something in her smile. "My work is the very private side of me." Taking off his hat and shaking off the snow, he looked around as if he had some twinge of apprehension.

"Please." When she smiled again, touching his arm so easily, her eyes kept saying: "Who can I go to if I can't go to you? You know this." Then meeting her eyes, he, too, smiled slowly as if admitting she had some moving claim on him. He said: "I'll tell you what we'll do, Lisa. Tonight after midnight—it may be even closer to one—I'll be crossing this intersection on my way home from my friend Hennessey's place." Then he laughed. "I may have had a few drinks too many."

"We've seen you, Mr. Shore."

"So you did. Not lurching, I hope."

"No. Navigating beautifully."

"I always do. But tonight I'll drink very little, I promise. If I'm home there'll be a light on over the door. Remember, it'll be past midnight. Tell your Al to drop by. Well, I leave you now. Wait. Don't cross at this corner with me. You might get hit on the way back. It's a bad corner. I'm used to it. Good night, Lisa."

"Mr. Shore—"

"Yes?"

"Thank you," she said softly, "Thank you very much." Warm with exultation she stood there watching him cross through the traffic. His head kept turning, his eyes on cars coming north, then turning to the cars from the south, then taking a swift glance over his shoulder at cars coming from behind and swerving around him.

73

11

At midnight a light was on over the door as Shore had said it would be. Up close in the light, the thick, paneled, heavy, black door had a shine as if it had just been rubbed up, but the brass-ware, the letter box, the doorknob and the knocker did not have the hard glossy shine of the brass on the house next door. Up close you could see that the big knocker was of dull, beaten brass. The keyhole was in the doorknob which was a heavy, old-fashioned, very worn, attractive piece of work. Just to the left on the brickwork was a bell button.

Al went to press this button. Then, keyed up as he was, he couldn't believe this solid door would open to him, so he reached for the knocker and pounded three times, waited a little, and was ready to pound again. Then the door opened. Shore said, "Al Delaney?"

"Al Delaney. Yes, sir."

"Well, come on in. I just got home," and he stepped back, and he was in the hall light in his brown jacket and blue slacks. His iron-gray hair was thinning. His eyes were soft, yet there was something tough in his face. Some would say he had a friendly garageman's manner; others would insist that he had a cool, lordly ease. His house wasn't what Al had expected. The walls were white, not brown. The whole house seemed to be done in white with flashes of color in the rugs and paintings. Al grinned nervously. Mr. Shore smiled gently.

"Now let me take your coat, Al," Mr. Shore said. He had the good-humored ease of an old friend. Leading Al into the library, he pointed to a tray on which there was a bottle of brandy. "Help yourself, Al. I've had enough." He sat down in a rocking chair by the window.

"Al Delaney," he said thoughtfully, his head on one side. "There was a fighter named Al Delaney, wasn't there?"

"It must have been before my time, sir."

"Just about before mine, too. A light heavyweight, if I remember. Miss Tolen is a beautiful girl, Al. A flame."

"I'll tell her, sir."

"Better not. She might decide to burn you up," and he laughed. "Well, how's that book coming along?"

"I've just about got it worked out."

"A book about my work. Hmmm. And who's going to be interested?"

"Students," Al said quickly. "And people like me." He was still a little afraid of Shore, but he went on confidently, "I have a hunch a lot of intelligent people are sick to death of politics and sociology and statistical wisdom and economics and all that crap that tells you nothing about life."

"Well, you could be right, I suppose."

"I'm dead right."

"Good. Then what do you make of those books of mine?"

"You disturb my sleep," Al said. "Love stories shouldn't upset me. But if love is its own law—hell—where does it go? No wonder people are afraid of love." Shore made no comment, listening gravely, as if Al himself was entitled to the greatest respect; and Al, in awe of that Shore insight that had enchanted him, wanted to blurt out: Why do these strange criminal minds fascinate you? What happened in some dark corner of your life? Was it something you regret bitterly not having done? Something that happened when you were young? A crime—a criminal very close to you? A violent, heart-breaking death? Was it around here? I've got it right, haven't I?

But he dreaded being answered; he had to believe with all his heart in his insight, so he started talking about the Shore work being unlike the work of any other writer he could think of. Camus, Chekhov, Borges— who was there? Other writers? Shore suddenly opened up. He had stories to tell about his contemporaries. He talked amusingly about Bellow and Mailer as if they were old neighbors. Al was enchanted. Shore seemed to come so close to him.

"There's this one big difference," Al said. "You make me look at my own life. The more I read you, the more life becomes a mystification."

"And the more I look at life," Mr. Shore said, shrugging, "the more of a mystification it becomes to me."

"No," Al said bluntly. "It's held together for you."

"It is?"

"Of course it is," Al said, but he felt suddenly pushed away again. "I—I sometimes wonder; why do you go on living in this town, Mr. Shore?"

"Where should I live?"

"Anywhere. Egypt, Paris, New York, the Bahamas."

"Why the Bahamas? I don't owe any income tax."

"But to bury yourself here?"

"Am I in exile in my home town?" he asked, his eyes full of gentle mockery. "Well, it may be that my town is like a monastery for me. Come to think of it," he went on, smiling ironically, "the editor of the *World* wants me to write a long feature article about my native heath. Anything I want to write as long as it sounds like me. Just take a look at anything in town. I may do it, too." He waved his well-shaped hand at the brandy. "Help yourself." Then he put down his pipe. "Al," he said gently, "I understand you've hit one of those terrible writing blocks."

"Block? Who said it was a block, Mr. Shore? Lisa?"

"Well, not a block—some difficulties."

77

"Of course there are difficulties. But really, they grow more exciting. My mind races, a world opens up—" He poured himself a big drink of brandy and gulped it down, trying to calm himself. It was so quiet now in the house. Outside, too, no noise; it was as quiet as a park in the dead of night, with Shore watching him and wondering. "A scholar rarely gets this kind of adventure out of his work." Al went on, feeling his way: "I had picked on Mailer. That over-the-windmill stuff, eh?" He told Shore about the European trip and his conversation with Marcus Stevens and about his performance with the Welsh poet in the Falstaff. "I started to read your work," he said awkwardly. "Something in it struck me. Something that I knew belonged to me. Well, I wrote thousands of words. I got bogged down. I wasn't getting at the right thing. . . ." Shore's eyes, taking in everything and telling nothing, began to upset him. Just as he was ready to blurt out, "The thing is, why the necessity of criminality?" Shore began to rock back and forth in the chair. The sound startled Al. . . . There was Shore, just as he had seen him in his vision, rocking and mocking him. "I've been fascinated discovering your characters all break the law—some kind of law, anyway," he said as if just speculating. "Maybe they have to do this to have their own being. That's it. Isn't that it?" Shore, uncommitting, went on rocking. "To have their own being?" Al said, his hand giving his beard a little pat. "So they can be free and independent with each other, even, I mean, to have any sense of justice about themselves." When Shore still didn't stop rocking, Al let the words flow out of him. "It's a big subject, I know. It's quite fascinating, isn't it? A man's sense of freedom, his love, his full love, maybe his independence. Does it always have to be put down?" Suddenly Shore was motionless in the chair, his eyes so alert that Al felt as big as he had felt that first night walking at night among the tall buildings. I've got it right, he thought. My God, have I got it right?

"I'll say one thing for you, Al," Shore said quietly.

"What's that?"

"You like criminals."

"That's not it."

"What is it, then?"

"What is it you live by?"

"What does a man live by?" Shore said, almost ill at ease. "No one asks that question nowadays, do they?" He was ready to draw back from some unexpected invasion of himself. "Do you read Starkey Kunitz?" he asked.

"Yes, sir."

"Kunitz doesn't look at me as you do."

"Kunitz was as baffled as I was, sir."

"Kunitz baffled? Never, Al," he said, smiling faintly. But the wary surprise remaining in his eyes made Al fumble at his words, and so Shore went on rocking in his chair, his unlighted pipe held out in one hand. His face too was inscrutable again. "I'm interested in faces," Al said, "People's lives in their faces. With your work in mind, I look at faces in the street. Night faces."

"Night faces?"

"Yes."

"Really?"

"I look at each face, wondering what they are really up to. Is there anything left to be up to or are they wards of the court, satisfied? Oh, I could go on." Laughing, he looked at his watch. "I wanted to see you, talk to you. I loved this, and now, my God, it's 1:30! There'll be another time, won't there, sir?"

"Wait, Al," Shore said, standing up slowly, his eyes on the floor as he hesitated. "Al, you're—" He paused, looking gravely at Al. Then asserting himself over the surprise he had shown, he took Al firmly by the arm. "I usually have a bite to eat before I go to bed," he said. "You're coming along with me. I'll get the car. Come on. It'll be on your way home." He got Al his coat and put on his own coat. Then they went along the hall and through the house, the dining room, the breakfast room, rooms in a graceful house full of brightness, and out to the garage where they got in the car.

They drove around the block to the intersecting streets where Lisa had left Mr. Shore, then down three blocks and across a block to Jarvis. They stopped in front of a big, brown-stone mansion that belonged to the old days in town. Not a light was in a window. In the heavy wet mist the old mansion looked desolate and abandoned. Shore led Al to a side door. He rang. A middle-aged, plump, smiling, dark-haired man in a dinner jacket opened the door. "Ah, Mr. Shore. Good evening," he said.

"Good evening, Alfred," Shore said. He was taking off his coat. The smiling doorman took their coats. Shore, his hand on Al's arm, led him up the thickly carpeted stairs to an oaken hall softly lit, then opened a door and they were in a small oak dining room with only six tables, shining with white linen tablecloths. The only other person in the room, a woman of 30, a blonde in a white evening dress, with an elegant air and love-ly tired eyes, sat at a corner table drinking a liqueur and wait-ing for someone with contented assurance—even at that hour. Though she hardly turned her head, her eyebrows moved. Al's beard and hair. Though she didn't turn again, Al thought the lifted eyebrows told him he didn't belong in this luxurious place.

"What a pleasant spot, Mr. Shore," he said, as they sat down. "Like a secret corner."

A maitre d', also in a dinner jacket, came in. "How are you, Mr. Shore?" he asked, as if they were old friends. He was the perfect maitre d', in charge, unhurried.

Then the small room and thick carpet and the one composed, beautiful, waiting woman began to unnerve Al.

"Well, let's see now, Al," Shore asked, paying no attention to the menu a waiter had brought. "Yes, I recommend the hare paté with toast tips, and I suggest we let Edgar put some brandy in your coffee. Eh, Edgar?" The maitre d', smiling reassuringly, left them. "I didn't know this town had places like this, Mr. Shore," Al said.

"The restaurant is downstairs, Al. I think it is closed now," Shore said as if he weren't sure. No, the place wasn't a club. No, it wasn't restricted. He had been coming there for years. The waiter brought the hare paté with the toast tips. It was delicious. "Are you drinking, Mr. Shore?" the waiter asked. "Yes, my Vichy water with the paté," Shore said. Vichy water with the paté! Then Al got the hang of the scene and quickened and had one of his hunches. He was suddenly sure that he, in his turn, had something Shore really wanted.

After he had lit a cigar, Shore began to question Al. He asked where he was born and about his family and what they had talked about in his home, and what he had read as a boy. Then, taking his time, he reflected on some of the answers, as if he had to place Al. Once he paused, looked idly at the young woman who remained so splendidly off by herself, then leaned back, studying the long ash on his cigar. Shore had a bemused air. "It's always strange to meet a young man who has his own perceptions," he said, half to himself. Then he shrugged. "I don't know, Al. I like this town. It's been just right for me. A place to be sure of. When I was in college, starting to write, nobody had any interest. Nobody around here had any interest in my first book. Well, that was fine. I had something to keep to myself. Another world—a world outside." He smiled, remembering. "I remember a man in New York saying to me, 'In that town of yours, Gene, who do you talk to about your work?' and I said, 'Why I talk to myself, of course.' Do you know something, Al?" and now he had a deprecating little laugh. "Tonight, listening and talking to you, I had a feeling I never expected to have in this town. I suppose I've been starving for years for some conversation about my own work."

It doesn't make sense, Al thought. Here he is comfortable and at ease in this town. Could it be that he looked down his nose on all the local cultural figures? A proud arrogant man?

"Come on, now, Al. I'll drive you home," Shore said. The waiter didn't bring a check. The maitre d', when they passed him, merely smiled and bowed. Shore was following Al, and when they were near the table of that pretty, well-groomed woman with the sensual lips, Al could see out of the corner of his eye that Shore in passing had caressed her upper arm, and she had touched his hand, patting it affectionately, intimately. Yet Shore had given no sign that he knew her.

81

It had begun to snow, heavy, slow-falling flakes in the mild, soft air, soft, spring, gentle snow, making the night lovely. When they got in the car they drove two blocks north and turned west. A mist seemed to hold the melting snow. Everything the headlights touched dissolved into a yellow glow. They stopped at Bay Street, waiting for the light to change. To the west were the floodlit towers of the government buildings, and farther downtown other floodlit towers hung in the air like golden balls. "Gold balls over a pawn shop," Shore said.

"So that's how you feel about this town," Al began, but a newspaper delivery truck had stopped at the intersection. A man ran to a corner newspaper-vending machine with a pile of morning papers and tossed them in the snow near the machine, then ran back to the truck which had hardly stopped.

"Just a minute, Al," Shore said and got out of the car and went over to the vending machine. Shore, his hand on his hip, looked down at the tied-up bundle in the snow. Al saw him stoop and extract a paper, and he saw him put his hand in his pocket then bend down again to the pile. Covered with wet snow he came hurrying back to the car and put the newspaper beside him on the seat. "I couldn't get to sleep at night if I didn't have the morning paper with me," he said and drove on, crossing the intersection.

Then they heard a car behind them honking. As Shore speeded up, the siren sounded. "What the hell is this?" Shore said.

When he had pulled over to the curb the police car was right behind them. Shore, lowering his window, waited until the cop appeared and leaned in. "What's the trouble?" Shore asked.

"Get out of the car. Both of you," the cop said.

"What is this?" Al said. It was snowing more heavily now, but they could see by the half-contemptuous expression on the big cop's handsome face that he was in a bad mood.

Al's beard seemed to interest, then satisfy, the cop but with the screen of snow between them, he couldn't tell whether Shore was an affluent man. Shore's car was neither big nor new.

This cop had learned that a poor man need not be treated with the respect you offered an affluent man. It could be assumed that all affluent men were on the side of the police. "If you'll be good enough, gentlemen," he said with routine politeness. "Go and get in the back seat of my car."

"What the hell is this?" Al said angrily.

"Take it easy, Al," Mr. Shore said, and they followed the cop and got into the back seat of the car and waited while he got in the front seat, flicked on the light and leaned over scrutinizing them. "Come on now, officer," Mr. Shore said impatiently.

"You were right under my eye at the intersection. I saw you take a paper," the cop said. "You didn't go near the box. Is this a habit of yours?"

"I *stole* that paper?"

"What do you call it? You guys never call it stealing, do you?"

"Well, now," Shore said, chuckling. "I know that thieving is a national pastime. . . ." Then suddenly alert, he said: "Why, you're serious! Officer, I assure you I paid for that paper."

"You didn't go near the box. Just took it from the bundle. I saw you."

"Did you see me leave the quarter?"

"What did you do? Toss it in the snow? Come on—"

"There's a wire around the bundle. I stuck a quarter under that wire." Then, angry but full of dignity, Shore leaned back. "Officer, I assure you I paid for that paper." When the cop, his face impassive, didn't answer, Shore said angrily: "Why don't you go back there and look?"

"You pick the right night to ask a guy to look" the cop said cynically. Then he smiled faintly. It was the first break in his wooden manner; he expected to give himself some pleasure. "Okay," he said, "we'll go back and look. Get in your car. I'll follow you. When you get out of the car, wait for me."

Back in his car, Shore took a long time turning on the ignition. Al went to speak but couldn't. He was sure that Shore, reflecting, was wondering if someone passing the bundle had seen the quarter and picked it up. Any kid passing, any bum would do it. The grim, humorless, sullen cop would surely get satisfaction out of charging him with petty theft—and there was Shore starting the car and turning back to try to prove that he wasn't a thief. Al began to be embarrassed. "Just let's hope it's there," Shore said. His smile bothered Al.

They came to the corner, got out, waited for the cop, and all marched across the road together. The pile of newspapers, snow-covered now, was there, but the wrapping wire was invisible. There were footprints near the bundle, and prints circling a little as if someone had stopped and then gone on. "Okay," the cop said, and Shore, crouching down, scraped the snow away. He brushed until the wire was visible. There, gleaming in the wet, was the quarter under the wire.

"Well, well, well," the cop said lightly. "You even left a tip. A big man."

Standing up slowly, Shore relaxed in relief, and then the indignity of the scene stung his pride. "Yes, that's a funny line," he said. "A comedian, I see. I'll bet you're known as the comic cop. Come on, Al."

The cop, standing there in the snow, let them walk across the road, but Al knew he followed them with his eyes, feeling insulted. Al wanted Shore to start the car and get away quickly. The cop came striding toward the car and banged on the window and when Shore lowered it he put his head in. "No one should drink and drive in his kind of weather. When I stopped you and you lowered the window the smell from the booze nearly knocked me over."

"I'm driving and I haven't been drinking," Shore said.

"I'm the one who was drinking," Al said.

"You must be one hell of a drinker then. This car still reeks of booze."

"The heater has been on. The window closed," Al said.

"You," the cop said to Shore. He waited, letting Shore look up at him. He waited at least 10 seconds. In the car light the cop's face was full of patient controlled contempt for this man who had called him a comedian. "You," he repeated. "Let me see your driver's license."

While Shore took out his wallet, searching uncertainly through the cards as if he hadn't been asked to show a driver's license in 40 years, the cop watched the fumbling fingers with a grim smile. "Get out of the car," he said finally as he took the license.

"This is outrageous," Shore protested, but he kept his dignity. He got out of the car. "Now what on earth do you want?"

"Open the trunk."

"Open the trunk? Why?"

"I said, open the trunk. Where's the key?"

Al, who had got out of the car, hoped Shore, who was approaching the rear of the car, would find the right key. He found it, but then, outraged at the indignities he was suffering, he whirled on the cop. "Why, you're giving me a drunkenness test?" But his words floated away in the snow, for as he whirled, his foot slipped on the slush. He fell to his knees and his hat rolled off. Al cried, "No, no Goddamn it," protesting half bewildered, because just a few hours ago in Shore's place they had been having a fine philosophical discussion about criminals, and here was Shore sprawled in the snow at the feet of this big cop.

"Mr. Shore," Al cried. "here." He helped Shore to his feet, then got him his hat. While Shore brushed the snow from his hat and adjusted it on his head, the cop waited calmly. Shaking his finger at the cop, Shore went to speak, but before he could say a word, the cop said: "Go on now. Open the trunk." For a moment Shore hesitated, staring at the cop, controlling himself, then obediently he opened the trunk. Not a word was said while the cop, using his flashlight, searched in every corner as if he had been tipped off that the trunk was laden with narcotics. When he had finished his search, he said: "Now close the trunk."

"Why, yes, I'll close the trunk," Shore said quietly. When he had done this, he faced the cop. "Enjoying every moment of

85

this, aren't you?" he said contemptuously. "The vindictive little cop. Well, I can't even feel sorry for you." The utterly savage contempt in Shore's voice and the way he drew back as if the cop were dirt surprised Al. He couldn't have taken this contempt himself. "Your little rule book entitles you to do this to me," Shore went on in disgust. "The law says that any pigheaded, mean cop can harass a citizen in this way—if he manages to keep a straight face doing it."

The cop couldn't seem to answer, and they were now two figures in the snow, facing each other, the falling snow a screen between their faces. Shore with his head back in lordly disdain and the cop, stiffening, growing tense, his head jerking back involuntarily. He was six inches taller than Shore. But now Shore, with contempt pouring out of him, was the commanding figure because he was so sure of himself.

"These things you do," Shore went on, "these ritual things, maybe they're a protection for me. If you didn't have them to fall back on, as the law probably knows, you'd blow your top, and God knows what you'd do, eh?" The cop's jaw was moving, his face ugly with rage. Then just for a moment he looked bewildered as if he felt this man in the snow could destroy him and surely would.

"Listen you," he said wildly and grabbed Shore by the arm. Al took two quick steps toward them. If the cop hit Shore, he knew he would hit the cop. He knew he couldn't help himself, and he didn't care. Holding Shore's arm, the cop struggled to control himself and remember his training—and he managed it. He relaxed, still staring at Shore. Then he said calmly: "So you've got a big mouth. Well, get into the car and turn on your brights."

"Well, of course," Shore said, sarcastically, and he got in the car and turned on his bright lights.

"Now the taillights," the cop called. When he had looked at the flashing taillights, he called again. "The brake lights; put your foot on the brake." He stood at the back of the car, Al beside him. Finally he came round to Shore. "Your left brake light isn't working," he said with satisfaction.

86

"Is that right, Al?"

"That's right, Mr. Shore."

"Driving a vehicle in imperfect condition in a snowstorm is dangerous. You should know better," the cop said flatly. He had held onto Shore's license and began to write a ticket.

"I won't pay this," Shore said quietly. "I'll go to court."

"Good," the cop said, handing him his license and the ticket.

"In court you won't be the big cop," Shore said. "When I'm finished with you, even the judge, even the court clerk, will look down on you. Understand?" But the cop was walking back to his own car. Al followed him.

Standing by the car with the door open and his face in the light, the cop looked powerful.

"Just a minute, officer," Al said politely. In his taxi-driving days Al had learned how to get along with cops. "I'm the witness," he said. "Take my name—Al Delaney. Here's my address," and he took his notebook out of his pocket, tore out a page, and wrote down the address. Drops of snow blurred his writing.

"Give it to the old guy," the cop said.

"What old guy?"

"That old guy."

"That's funny," Al said, starting to laugh. "You know who he is?"

"Go on home. Your beard's getting wet."

"I know a guy like you doesn't read. . . ."

"I can read, smartass."

"Terrific," Al said. "You're a reader. Keep it up," and he laughed again. "That old guy's Eugene Shore. I think you're gonna read about yourself in the papers."

The cop snorted, but when Al shrugged, as if he didn't care, the cop hesitated, staring back at Shore sitting in the car. It was as if the threat the cop had felt in Shore's contempt touched him again or as if he were wishing he hadn't given him that ticket. Suddenly apprehensive, he went to speak, but Al, turning away, walked back to the car and got in beside Shore.

As they drove along, Al said nothing. He couldn't; he felt too keyed up. He could still see those two hostile figures facing each other tensely in the snow. He still felt the need in him to hurl himself on the cop's back if he had assaulted Shore, and he was bewildered by the exhilaration these feelings gave him.

"Al, I'm sorry about all this," Shore said evenly, "but I hate everything that man stands for."

"I can see you do," Al said, and they both laughed. "In the morning this unexpected snow will be gone," Shore said, "and the whole thing will seem ridiculous."

"My place is just three houses beyond the next stop—on the right," Al said. When they had made the turn he tried furtively to get a glimpse of the expression on Shore's face as the street lights flickered over it. He could feel the ease in Shore now as he sat beside him. My God, he's tough. Secretly so tough, he thought. Yet this man's work was full of compassion and tenderness. No compassion whatever for the cop. Maybe in his own way he was even tougher than the cop if it came to protecting his own domain. But *what* did he think was his own domain?

Now I see it, he thought suddenly. I've been barking up the wrong tree. Criminals. Criminals. Shore could be a little crazy. All things just reversed for him. To him that cop was a criminal. All the big law-and-order men the real criminals. He hated tham all. Cops of the courts, cops of the church, political cops. Society's cops. All to be kept out of his domain, and who the hell could be in that domain except, maybe the artist and the saint, the last of the outlaws, holed up in the hills in some fine and private place? Could Lisa be there, Al wondered. Shore liked her. Suddenly he gave an awkward laugh that startled Shore.

"I was just thinking," Al said. "Why have I always been able to get along with cops? Too long with that damn taxi, I guess. Maybe it's the graduate school training, the academic, the artist's cop, eh? The graduate school, a big cop shop, eh?" Then he blurted out recklessly: "This book I'm doing on you . . . the academic coming after you to pin you down, put the handcuffs on you." But Shore, bursting out laughing, cut him off. "That's very good, Al," he said. "Well, here we are," and he stopped the car.

In the headlights the road ahead was a black, glittering strip. There was now a thin rain. Gobs of melting snow plopped from tree branches to the sidewalk. There was a light in Lisa's window.

"You and Lisa live up there, eh?" Shore said. "Lisa's a very interesting girl," and he leaned across Al trying to see the lighted window but couldn't. He couldn't see the figure there, Lisa waiting and wondering. Al did not say, "Look, she's up there at the window now"; he didn't want Shore to be more interested in Lisa than he was in Al. "Well," he began, "this has been a wonderful evening for me. I'll remember it for a long time."

"Me too," Shore said, leaning back comfortably, his gloved hands on the wheel. "I liked meeting you, Al."

"Good night, Mr. Shore."

"Just a minute."

"Yeah, Mr. Shore?"

"Why can't we have dinner tomorrow night? My wife is out of town. You and Lisa join me."

"We'd love to."

"The King Edward, eh? I still like that old Victoria room. 7:30 in the lobby?

"We'll be there—and again, many thanks."

"Good night, Al."

Al got out of the car and stood there watching it go up the street, then he hurried in and up the stairs to the light at the top where Lisa waited.

"That was Shore, wasn't it? And you've been with him all this time, and he drives you home."

"With him? Oh, you bet. Lisa, it was a wild evening," and he threw off his coat, laughing exuberantly, then made her follow him into the living room and wait and watch him. She was in her black-and-brown, silk housecoat which was undone, her throat and chest and shoulders were bare, and in this half-naked elegance she searched his face while he smiled broadly.

Then she saw that his beard was wet, and his hair too and his shoes looked as if he had been walking in puddles. "Come on, Al," she said. "What have you been doing? Rolling in the snow?"

"Just about."

"Come on. Come on."

"Sit down. It's really very funny," he said, and he drew her down beside him. He told her what had happened. He gave her every little detail right from the moment when he had pounded on Shore's door to the scene in the snow. Then he chuckled. "Imagine, Lisa. Shore nearly gets charged with petty thievery. Can't you see that in the newspapers?" But she, off by herself, said softly, "Imagine. Hare paté on toast tips."

"With Vichy water."

"With Vichy water. I like that."

"Have we still got that bottle of brandy we got in the Paris airport?"

"It's on the top shelf of my closet in the bedroom."

"What have we been saving it for?"

"Why, for this occasion. Right?"

"Right," he said. "I'll get it." He got up, feeling wonderfully warm and relaxed, but at the door he stopped, pondering, then he said, "I'll tell you a funny thing."

"What's that?"

"You thought I had Shore all wrong, didn't you?"

"I didn't say that."

"Come on. That was the idea."

"No, I thought you couldn't make your mind up about what your view of him was, and that if you met him. . . ."

"No, I had him right, Lisa. He's all that, only more so. The funny thing is, I knew it when I wanted to jump on that cop's back and feel the whole human race cheering me on. Shore's a tiger, Lisa. A hidden tiger," and he laughed and turned to go into the bedroom.

Then he heard her say, "What's the matter with tigers? I always liked tigers," and he turned back. Her face was so full of warm glowing satisfaction that he was deeply moved and couldn't take his eyes off her. Her head back, her eyes not on him now, she nursed her satisfaction with a little dreaming smile. Then suddenly she giggled. "I was just thinking—" She paused, reflecting, making him wait. Then she giggled again. "The other night, talking about your work, I said, Where is the cop? Well, here he is, I guess."

12

In the hotel lobby Shore, in his beautifully cut, double-breasted suit with the chalk stripe, put out his hands, his wrists flashing two inches of white cuff with monogrammed gold cuff links. He led them into the elegant, old-fashioned dining room. Al had brought along a book for Shore to sign. Shore's manner was so amiable that by the time they had ordered drinks, he was like an old friend. Studying the menu, he said: "Let's have a good feed."

Al had put the book down on the floor by his chair. Now he picked it up, "Remember this one?" he asked.

"Oh, indeed I do. Well, well," Shore said, looking at the book. "This book really did big things for me," he said fondly. "Do you remember the sportswriter, old Wilf Barnaby? A man with lucrative sidelines. This old pirate was a friend of my friend Sam Ivey, the fight promoter. Sam, who once said he would steal a stove if he could carry it away, was a great-hearted man. I liked him. When Barnaby died suddenly, Sam Ivey, collecting tributes for a memorial banquet in the sports world, asked me to write something. Brooding over Barnaby, a corrupt man, all I could remember was Barnaby saying, 'There's no such thing as a dirty dollar!' "

But later he recalled a night when Sam Ivey had given him a ticket to the Clay–Chuvalo fight and told him to sit with the press at ringside. Men claiming to be sportswriters turned up with credentials from trade journals, the plumbers' manual, women's wear, the builder's guide, and so on. "The newspapermen couldn't get seats, and old Barnaby, in a rage, cursed the interlopers. The head usher came, bouncing them out of the seats, myself included."

Shore said: "I told them to see Sam Ivey, but he couldn't be found. I was pulled out of the seat next to Barnaby's. 'Wait a minute,' Barnaby said to the usher. 'Eugene Shore? Are you the guy who wrote the book about the two hookers and the priest?' Then he said to the usher: 'This guy is a real writer, and he's entitled to sit by me.' Then he mumbled half to himself: 'I'm not going home and tell my wife I let them throw out the guy who wrote that book she liked so much. I want to get some sleep tonight.'"

Chuckling, Shore said: "You see why I like that book, Al?"

"I like it, anyway," Al said. "By the way, I sent those two books you autographed to my brother in California. I wondered if you'd autograph this one for my father." He told him he felt he had been unfair to his father, in falling out with him.

"Wait a minute," Shore said dubiously. "If that's the case, I don't think I'd send this book to your father."

"Why not?"

"Not if you want to mollify him. Not as a sympathetic gesture."

"I thought it might make him wonder about things."

"Do you want to upset him again? He might think you did it on purpose, that you're not close to him at all."

"Well, maybe," Al said, reflecting. "Yes, I think I'd trust your judgment," and he put the book back. Changing the subject, he asked if Shore remembered him talking about Marcus Stevens in Rome, then the scene in the Paris bar. "You know something, Mr. Shore?" he said. "You brought out the phony in me."

"Now Al—"

"Al's no phony," Lisa said calmly.

"No, he's not," Shore agreed. "I think I know a lot about Al." But his eyes, going to Lisa, dwelt on her full breasts where the dress tightened at the breast line. Al saw that Lisa had caught Shore's glance. Indeed she had met Shore's eyes, smiling faintly. Half upset and wondering, Al remembered how much she had been aware of the look Shore had given her, meeting her for the first time outside his door. And now this glance from Shore at her breasts seemed to be a further approving recognition of more of her, as he had remembered her in the beginning. The approval was still there in Shore's face, and Al looked at it, quickening as if it could tell him things about Lisa he hadn't found out himself. This smooth, calm ruddy face could have been the face of a judge. Mr. Justice Shore. Chancellor Shore. Or better still, Bishop Shore. That big nose would poke around in dark places. A nose for young women. Maybe in Mexico, Paris, New York—secret places far from home. The seventeenth-century divines would be fascinated by the nose, Al thought, in his scholarly fashion. Noses and ears, all that had been left for the divines to look at?

But Shore, refilling the wine glasses, then moving a spoon in a slow circular motion on the white tablecloth, meditated. "I've thought about it, Al," he said finally. "I'm satisfied you'll do something pretty good."

"Really?"

"Yes."

"May I ask something?" Al said.

"Go ahead."

"Until now," Al said, "you've been content to be as anonymous as one of those old sculptors who worked on the Cathedral at Chartres. You know how it was. Living only in the light their work cast on them. And now. . . ."

"Maybe I'd like to see myself in the light you put me in," Shore said, shrugging. "I know it'll be interesting. So if I can do anything to help you get off on the right foot—"

"I'm sure you can," Lisa said quickly. Leaning closer, her lovely face was full of soft, cunning, seductive eagerness. Her

95

long necklace swung across her breast.

"Lisa," Al said, "just give me a chance." Startled, she leaned back, thinking she had misunderstood him. "Can I be blunt, Mr. Shore?" Al asked.

"Go ahead."

"You wear these double-breasted suits. Right now, you look like the chairman of the board. In your neighborhood you're surrounded by brokers and coupon-clippers, and you seem to be right at home with them. Excuse me, I meant"—he stammered: "Now that you've come into the limelight, has anything changed?"

"Yes," Shore said, smiling. "I've been invited to sit around some night at the university and talk to the students."

"Are you going to?"

"No."

"Is that all?"

"Well, the editor of the *Evening World* has asked me to do a long article for the Sunday supplement about this, my town. Anything I want to write is okay with them."

"Why don't you do it?"

"What could I hang it on?"

"Does something have to stir you up?"

"Why write or talk about anything if you're not stirred up?"

"I'd like to see you do it. It'll be a headline."

"I don't need a headline."

"You are now—you should be, too."

"The thing is, Lisa," Shore said, turning to her mockingly, "I think Al wonders why I haven't reached for a headline by stabbing my wife in the belly, why I haven't put on big alcoholic scenes in bars. Right, Al? Wrestled lions in Africa?" He snorted with contempt. "For what? To be loved here as a big public personality? What would it make me?"

"The town whore, I suppose," Lisa said brightly.

"Exactly, Lisa."

"Just the same, you're strange fruit for this town," Al said doggedly. "I can't figure out where you come from."

"Where I come from?" Shore repeated, utterly baffled. "Good God. What is it you want of me?" When Al didn't answer, he went on gently. "Why are your eyes brown, Al? Why do birds fly south and not get lost? Why did Lisa come your way?"

A flush on his face, staring at Shore obstinately, Al kept saying with his eyes: *Open up, Mr. Shore. Open up.*

"I do my parables; I see little things happening," Shore went on. "I try and get them down. Maybe then some nut comes along and talks about symbols. Symbols? The whole thing is the symbol. The whole thing. If there's any magic it's in the way the imagination holds a life together. Yours as well as mine, Al. Maybe I see something in a bar or a cathedral. Maybe a man tells me a little story . . . something happening that bothers him. Now take my book. . . ."

Leaning closer to Lisa, watching the changing expressions on her warmly inviting face, he quickened or slowed the rhythms of his story as her expression changed or her eyes shone or she burst out laughing. Al noticed that in telling stories about everything and everyone, Shore still told nothing about himself. And then it was ten o'clock. Waiters were hovering around. Those two tall, gray-haired, puffy-eyed, rich lawyers passing the table on the way out, Barnes and Orliffe, bowed to Mr. Shore, appraising him and the company he was in without any of the old familiarity. They had read about him in the newspapers. "Hello there," Shore called cheerfully. The men only bowed again. "Now what did I do to them, I wonder?" Shore said.

"Two of your fans?" Al asked.

"I went to law school with them," he said, his eyes turning inward. Then himself again, he said with a contented sigh: "Well, I've enjoyed this, but I've got to get home. In an hour my wife calls from Mexico."

"I'm obliged to you, Mr. Shore. Much obliged," Al said. "Maybe your wife is the one I should talk to now."

"Well, talk to her, Al."

"When?"

97

"In a month or so."

At the checkroom, when Shore was getting his hat, Al said, "I had the wild idea you might be able to come over to the Riverboat with us and listen to Sonny and Brownie. Come into our life a little, Mr. Shore."

"If that's your life, I've been in it for some time. They're as old as I am, aren't they?" he asked, smiling. "I've been to the Riverboat."

They stood for a moment at the hotel entrance. Across the road two men and a statuesque blonde were going into a bar, the woman holding hands with both men. Passing the entrance in a slow shuffling walk was a man with a funny, square, Russian hat, glasses and straggly gray hair hanging over his collar. He looked like an impoverished beaten up immigrant. The old fellow, staring blankly, shuffled by.

"Oh dear God," Shore said. "That's Wilfred Greenburg, the musician. I didn't recognize him." It was incredible, he said, but at college he had been at a party where Greenburg had played. He remembered a strip-poker game later, when Greenburg had got down to his underwear. It had been in the summer, but Greenburg had worn long johns. In recent years they hadn't met. "Now he passes me," Shore said, "and I don't even recognize him. Why is he suddenly so old—no, so alien? Is this what life has done to him?" Then he smiled wryly. "The joke may be on me, eh? The fact is, he didn't recognize me either, did he?" Squeezing Al's arm encouragingly, he said, "Well, go to it, Al. Good night, Lisa."

"Good night," she said softly and put her hands on his shoulders and kissed him in the European style, once on each cheek. Drawing back, he looked at her strangely with that same twinge of apprehension he had had the night she had stopped him on the street.

"Look, Al, I know it's sometimes hard to get off on the right foot," he said. "Why don't you let me see your first chapter? Call me, why don't you?"

"Oh, no. That would be an awful imposition."

"Not at all. Good night."

"Good night, it was great, Mr. Shore."

"Good night, Lisa," Mr. Shore called, walking to the curb. The doorman opened a taxi door.

"Isn't he a beautiful man?" Lisa said. "Al, you've got it made with him."

"Oh, sure."

"And you know something else? He goes for me."

"They all go for you, don't they?"

"This is different—I can tell," she said. "I know."

"What the hell did you say to him, Lisa?"

"Say when?"

"The night you went to see him."

"Just about the book."

"You told him I had a block. Goddamn it, Lisa. This is impossible. Am I a cripple?"

"Al, I love you."

"Okay. Just let things be."

"The way it is now, he'll even work with you."

"I'll do my own work."

"He'll help."

"I don't need his help. I have to know things he can't know."

"Alright, Al," she said and snuggled against him, enveloping him in the warmth of her affection, shaming him. But even here he had another quickening insight. What would happen to the artist in Shore if the public loved him as Lisa loves me? "Wait," he said. "I forgot the book."

"It's only a paperback," she said, but he turned back to the dining room.

A smiling waiter handed him the book. He hurried back to Lisa.

"My mind is in a whirl," he said. "Come on."

His arm around her waist, he walked her across the street to the parking lot. Stopping, he looked around. Then suddenly he wanted to be alone with his racing thoughts. "Do you realize, Lisa, that within a few blocks of here Shore roamed around when he was a student? His first stories came out of the life

99

around here. His lawbreakers, was he one of them? Something hit him hard right around here, not later on in Rome or Paris or Mexico. *Here,* Lisa! I could walk through this neighborhood and walk through his life."

"What else have you been doing night after night?"

"Walking through his books. Now that I know him—the strange things that happened to him must have happened around here. I'd like to look around by myself. You get some sleep."

"I don't sleep now if you're not beside me."

"I know," he said. "Isn't it the same with me?" He watched her get into her car and back out, the tail light vanishing around the corner. As he walked west alone, all his perceptions seemed to quicken. Soon he was passing places where Shore had walked and worked as a young man. He thought he could feel within himself the beginnings of that young man. But the doors that had opened and closed on Shore, the restaurants where he had sat, were gone. Torn down. Great glass and concrete towers there instead! At night it was a new town of floodlit empty towers and deserted streets. Office workers had fled for the night. Yet in the city's floodlit golden glow of empty, glassy towers, with the old City Hall clock tolling the hour—a quarter after ten—Al's imagination soared. He was back on that path that Starkey Kunitz had opened up into the world's universities, the path Kunitz could pursue no further himself in his bafflement. Yet he—Al Delaney—could go on. The scholarly world would have to turn to him, the greatest living authority on Eugene Shore. He saw how timely were the questions: In a world full of criminals who is the criminal? Priests, bank robbers, bank managers, hookers. Strange criminals who brought the vast host of respectable criminals against them.

Al turned along Queen, passing the floodlit split silo of City Hall and the shining pool in the great square and going on west to the law school. There it was, back of the wide lawn behind the great high old iron fence. Al imagined that he could see Shore, the law student, coming out of the shadows of an entrance and down the path to the antique gate in the iron fence. Was that fence there to keep people away from the law? Or to keep the law away from the people? A man studies law to learn that men cannot live on the law's empty satisfactions. The iron fence around the heart.

Turning east to the neighborhood of the young Shore and his early stories, he was soon in the roominghouse district around the cathedral, where the church spire, floodlit now, too, threw a light over streets that had been shadowy and mysterious for the young Shore.

"Enough. I've had it for tonight," he said wearily. He turned back to Yonge and north into the loose, idle, sprawling neighborhood under the neon signs. It was the first warm spring night. Al loafed along in the crowd. He was now in the neighborhood of hamburger joints, bars with naked-breasted girls, bars with naked-bottomed girls, dance halls, horror movies, dirty-book stores, Oriental shops and bazaars, and on the corner the hookers and pimps. Down the street in single file came eight young Buddhists in saffron robes and shaven heads, chanting, 'Krishna, Krishna.' Just behind them was a tall young fairy with ash blonde hair, mincing prettily, having such fun with the smirking jokers in the doorway. A girl brushed against Al. A young girl, a prostitute with a jaunty cap and a short skirt—oh, pretty, pretty. She went gaily down the street, circling toward one man, then another in a cheerful, slow, weaving, spring dance. She came back again, brushing against Al.

"I like your cap," he said. "It's a great cap."

"Not another one like it," she said.

"Yes, there is."

"Where?"

"In Paris. I saw a colleague of yours wearing one just like it."

"Paris, eh? Come with me and I'll take you right back to Paris—a ten-minute trip."

"I'm late," he said.

"Okay," she said cheerfully and moved on.

Another hooker was standing sedately in a doorway in a long white coat. It was her gesture at being alone and forlorn, yet she was getting a customer ahead of the gayer one. A big solemn man, joining her, followed her around the corner. But right behind her came the laughing pretty little one with a young man who had got out of a car after a bit of haggling.

Al headed for the brightly lit restaurant across the road from the big department store. A cop, coming out of this restaurant, was pushing two girls toward his car. One of them, tall, big-breasted, and handsome, was giving him a piece of her mind. The other one, a pert, neat, little girl, got into the car. "Come on, Mable," she said with lofty indifference. "Why waste your time?" But the cop had noticed that Al, now only a few feet away, was staring at him. Al started to laugh. Paying no attention, the cop opened his car door.

"It's you," Al said, smiling. "How are you?"

"Come on, move along," the cop said gruffly.

"Al Delaney. Don't you remember?"

"I don't forget so easy. The smartass witness."

"The *witness*. That's right. How's the reader? Still turning those pages?"

"Sure, the hookers turn tricks and I turn pages." The cop was grinning, and Al realized he was not so easily needled, that he had a very sure sense of himself.

"Say goodnight to the ladies," he said to Al, making him feel that somehow he'd been outmaneuvered. The cop was in the front seat, and as the car moved away slowly from the curb, Al leaned in the open window. "Here. Try this one," he called, tossing the book on the cop's knees. "It's all about this neighborhood." The car kept going.

Now why in hell did I do that? Al asked himself. He stood at the curb, trying to get used to his surprise.

13

Jason Dunsford took the book home. He lived with his pretty, freckled wife Helen in a four-room apartment in a new high-rise in the suburbs. Helen liked reading; she had a friend who was a librarian. As soon as Jason put his key in the door he had that sense of apprehension that had become a part of his life. Helen was an alcoholic, and he felt that it was his fault. A cop has crazy hours.

He had wanted to be an engineer, but when he was in high school his father, a typesetter in a printing shop, had died. Jason had left school to support his mother and two younger sisters. In his first two years on the police force, dreaming of quick promotion, he had seen himself someday becoming a master criminologist. But his real zeal and unyielding sense of rectitude had got him into trouble with his colleagues who thought he took himself and his job too seriously. They took him aside and explained that a man had to live and let live. Important people ought not to be brought against him. They said this because he had almost got Inspector Higgins fired by testifying that he had been present when the amiable, well-liked inspector had fixed some traffic tickets for an old newspaper friend. His colleagues resented having to watch themselves when Jason was around. Finally Jason understood that no one gave a damn about his scruples, so he became a routine cop, a grimly quiet, disappointed cop who secretly nursed the dangerous feeling that he was being overlooked. Yet he had never beaten up a prisoner who hadn't first assaulted him. He had learned how to take abuse. He had cultivated an effective, aloof, magisterial manner and a blunt, direct manner of speech. "A cop gets to know people at their lowest level," he would say to his friend, Ira Mustard. "I try to keep this in mind." Jason did not lose his temper when he was called a "pig" at student demonstrations. He had too much contempt for these students who had a chance at everything he had once wanted. As the years passed he had come to despise the public.

He came home this morning as he did every morning, hoping to come into the presence, the good memories, of the intelligent girl who had been his boyhood sweetheart. A policeman and his friends were an isolated group. A policeman couldn't freely make friends. Helen didn't like bridge parties and bowling tournaments and sports events. If she was at a party, Jason couldn't bear to see her leaning against some big cop so she wouldn't fall down, or lurch around, saying something shameful. They had cut out the parties. But Helen's only close friend, the librarian, Mollie Downs, a shy, sweet, intelligent girl, was a secret drinker. She often stayed with Helen all night. Before turning the key, Jason, standing with the book in his hand, dreaded that he might hear voices, one of them Mollie's. Then, as he always did, he steadied himself, wanting Helen as soon as he walked in to look at him and believe, no matter how much of a sot she might have made of herself, that she could draw on his strength and concern.

He opened the door. His big standard poodle came jumping all over him. Jason had learned that the most effective protection against burglars was not a cop but a dog, so he got the big poodle. The landlord told him that he would have to get rid of the dog because it had a temperamental hatred of anyone wearing a uniform. At first Jason couldn't even wear his policeman's outfit in his own house. However, he handled the problem patiently. In a sense he cunningly crept up on the poodle. For a few days he wore only his policeman's boots in the house; after a few days he wore the pants of the uniform; next day he added the shirt. The big day came when he added the cap, and there he was in full uniform, and the poodle hadn't noticed the change.

While Jason stroked the dog's head he listened for sounds that would tell him Helen was stirring. Tiptoeing into the bedroom, he saw her there, sleeping; then, feeling ashamed as he always did, he went a little closer and sniffed, the old terrible tension was in him. But when her eyes flickered open he smiled.

"Hello, Jason," she mumbled sleepily, one blue eye on him, one clear eye that satisfied him. "Put on the kettle, will you?" she asked, stretching. "I'll be right up."

"Take your time, little one," he called, going into the kitchen. He got eggs and bacon from the refrigerator so she could cook them for him. He began to sing. As a boy he had been in the church choir. He was singing when she came into the kitchen in her dressing gown, but he stopped to watch her scratching her head with both hands and screwing up her face, and he laughed. She looked like a young girl.

"How was last night?" he asked when she gave him his glass of orange juice. "Anything new?"

"I watched television and read. No phone calls. I had a very good evening, Jason. Anything new with you?"

"Nothing new. No," and then he got the book he had brought home. "Tell me something. Does the name Eugene Shore mean anything to you?"

"Shore? Eugene Shore! Isn't he a writer?"

"That's it. That's the guy."

"There was something about him in the papers a while back. An editorial, too, I think."

"I gave him a ticket the other night."

"So what?"

"How big is he in this town, Helen? Do you think he'd have connections? I'm tired of trouble."

105

"I remember Mollie talking about him. He made some kind of big splash. Why?"

"Nothing. He tried to look down his nose. That's all, honey. Just wanted to know if you had ever heard of him. Here's a book of his." He told her how he had got it. But something else was on his mind. "Look, Helen, a guy at the station asked me who I was called after. Jason! Who is Jason?"

"What? You're Jason."

"I mean the first one."

"He chased after the golden fleece."

"What's a fleece?"

"I think it was a piece of gold lamb's wool."

"All wool and a yard wide," and he grinned. "Well, you read the book."

"I think I will," she said, thumbing through the book. "Yes, it looks interesting. Maybe I'll read it tonight."

That night, on the beat, he liked thinking of her sitting at home reading. In the morning, when he came in, she had his breakfast ready and she was herself, beautifully herself. "That's a very moving story," she said thoughtfully. "The two hookers and the priest. Jason, it's a kind of spiritual thing, yet it's a love story. I used to be so interested in such things. Remember? Remember how I always had the lead in the high school plays? Wasn't it fun? And the skit I wrote. It couldn't have been as funny as they thought it was. And I was always talking to you about a book I had read, wasn't I? It all seemed so desperately important." But his silence flustered her. "What was I saying? Oh, yes. This story. Well, it comes down to a very interesting clash between the bishop and the priest. It all happens downtown. In the neighborhood you know so well. Your beat. Which was why I was quite moved. I'm not kidding. You should read it."

"Why?"

"You'll recognize things."

"Okay, maybe I'll read it."

Jason was sure Shore wouldn't know much about the

downtown neighborhood. It took him three days to read the book. He was not accustomed to reading fiction, but he wanted to be able to say, "This fool doesn't know what he's talking about." Reading so slowly, he began to believe every word. Just before dinner, when he finished the book, he sat back pondering. "I didn't think there was anyone in the world who could get sentimental about a couple of hookers," he said with a contemptuous laugh. "That priest was a kook, Helen. His bishop should have gone after him with a butterfly net."

"I thought he did."

"That's right. He did. Good for him."

"It's a good true story, isn't it, Jason?"

"Oh, come on, Helen. It's all bleeding-heart stuff," Jason said, laughing contemptuously. Yet he sat there, the book on his knee, beginning to brood, for in the back of his mind, as he read, had been the picture of Shore slipping to his knees in the snow, then rising to heap belittlement on him. It had been very gratifying to him to see in the story that Shore was on the side of rascally, wrong-headed priests against their bishops, and whores and pimps too. Of course it would be so. That angry man denouncing him in the snow, hating him there in the snow, had been an obvious cop-baiter, one of those secret enemies of the law. Putting that together with the stuff he had written in this book, maybe a man who wanted to be a criminal and just didn't have the guts to come into the open. That man would not show up in court. Men like him thought it over and paid their little fines out of court.

Then Jason found himself listening to Helen moving around in the bedroom. Each sound she made disturbed him more. Something in this Shore book had got under his skin, and these sounds from Helen made this thing a kind of personal resentment which was deepened by his recollection of Shore's contempt for him. The priest in the book—Shore's priest—had a lot of concern for the two hookers—loving concern and not much else. The fool didn't think he needed anything else.

The point of the book, as Jason saw it, was that this priest

107

had been such a big fool. His big concern hadn't given him any power over the girls or anyone else. The girls, not exactly kissing him off, had gone on with their shabby lives, and so the bishop had had to hit the priest on the head. Good for the bishop! Someone had to have some sense. But in spite of his cynical contempt for the priest, Jason, with Helen there moving around, began to think of his own loving concern for her, and then he felt sure that Shore, if he knew the situation, might now be pitying him as he had pitied the priest for imagining that his watchful love for Helen could keep her away from the bottle. This put him on edge; again he could hear Shore, half hidden in the falling snow, heaping contempt on him. What's the matter with me? he thought. He knew he ought to have arrested Shore for resisting an officer. Any inspector, any magistrate, would tell him he was right in arresting him and taking him to the station and booking him. Any officer would have been applauded by the authorities for not taking that abuse. What had been the matter with him? He couldn't believe he had felt some threat in Shore, but he began to squirm. That man could have been convicted. Then he would be where he belonged, a man with a record.

"Jason," Helen called, "isn't it time to take Percy out?" The big poodle, having come over to him, was eyeing him.

"Okay," Jason said, "okay."

At the end of the week Helen told him that Mollie was coming to dinner. It was alright with him. When he came home, he called: "Helen, Helen." She wasn't in the house. The bed hadn't been slept in. He collapsed in a chair. The poodle, circling around him, kept licking his hand. "Why didn't you keep that librarian lush out of this house?" he said to the poodle. "What good are you, Percy?"

He felt the beginning of panic; it could get worse, he knew, if he sat there waiting and hoping.

It was half past nine; he was still in uniform. He went out, moving like a slow, calm policeman and got in his own car. He drove downtown to the neighborhood near the central library.

Each time he had made this trip—and he had made it many

108

times—he told himself he wouldn't care if he did it a thousand times. Now for the first time, he dreaded going to Mollie's apartment.

Mollie lived on the second floor in an old house. Jason hated every step. He rapped on the apartment door. No one answered. Three times he rapped, then coldly sure of himself he crashed his big body heavily against the door. A bit of wood splintered off the door jamb.

The living room had a sour smell, mainly of alcohol. The drapes on the window were drawn. Helen was lying on the floor, her mouth open as she snored. The loud, gurgling snore shocked him. Looking down at her, Jason trembled, then he went to the window, threw back the drapes, opened the window, and turned and lifted his wife. Vomit was on the front of her dress. A dirty woman with stinking breath. He went into the bathroom, got a towel, soaked it in warm water, cleaned the dress, then gently wiped Helen's face until her eyes flickered and opened. "Is that you, Jason?" she said.

"It's alright. It's me," he said. Her bewildered blue eyes were pleading and frightened. Kissing her gently, he smoothed her golden hair. "It's alright," he said and touched the freckles on her face as he used to, reassuring her. When he had propped her in the corner of the couch she said woozily, "What time is it? Have you had your breakfast?" But he had heard Mollie snoring in the bedroom, a heavy rattling snore suddenly cut off. He took three firm strides to the bedroom and closed the door carefully.

Mollie had rolled off the bed and was getting to her feet, trying to push her hair back. "Jason," she pleaded, "look, Jason, please. You have such crazy hours. What's a woman to do? No, not just a few crazy hours, working hours, it's all the hours. It gets very lonely for her. Boring. When it gets that you can't stand it any longer, what do you do? People have to find a way of being together. I love Helen as much as you." Her hand came out suddenly, protesting, "Jason, wait a minute—"

He slapped her so hard that he knocked her down. She lay there whimpering, then got to her knees and crawled away from him to the wall, afraid he would kick her. "Now keep out of my life," he said quietly. He went back to the living room.

On the way home, while Helen dozed, her head against his shoulder, Jason sat stiff and stern, his big shoulders hunched up powerfully. He tried to tell himself that his suffering didn't matter; it had to be endured.

When they got to the apartment house he was glad there was no sunshine, nothing to bring the women and children out onto the street. It was a dull, dark morning, the sky full of rain. In the sunlight women would have been there with baby carts; children would be playing. Now the women could only watch from the window as they had watched other times. Mrs. Shevitz was there at her second-floor window. The curtain had moved. Getting out of the car, Jason held Helen's arm in such a tight grip, hurrying, that she seemed to be walking briskly into the apartment house to the security of their own place. The poodle, recognizing the step, was barking cheerfully, and when Jason opened the door it came at them with a loving leap, then followed Helen to the chair by the window. While the dog licked her hand, she went on running her fingers under its jaw. "Jason," she said brokenly, her white, sick face full of remorse.

"Can I get you anything, Helen? Some coffee?"

"Yes, coffee, Jason."

"Helen—"

"I'm sorry, Jason," she whispered, turning her head away. "I never told lies, did I, Jason? Now on the phone I make up stories about everything. I don't know why. Somebody phones me and I have a wild story to tell."

"This is no good. I've been a fool, Helen. I'm not helping you. It won't work. I can't make it work. You need to go away for a cure."

"I only need you with me, Jason."

"That's what I've made you think, Helen. I've been very foolish."

"Oh no. All I need is you, Jason."

"I don't do any good, Helen. It may even be a bad thing," he said, his words hurting him painfully. "Well, I'll get the

110

coffee. You know, I haven't had any breakfast." In the kitchen he made a pot of coffee. He liked the smell of it. It was important that coffee still had such a good smell. He took a cup to Helen. Her hand, holding the cup, trembled, and in that trembling hand and the way she looked up blankly was all the faith he had in the strength of his own loving concern and her belief that it was all she too needed. But he saw it all fading away— there in her face. He wanted to cry out, Why shouldn't it be enough? and had to turn from her. "Take off that dress," he said firmly. "We'll send it to the cleaners. A lot of things need to be cleaned up around here. Helen, you are going away."

"Jason! No!"

"Some real care and a real cure. Now it's up to you. *You.*"

"Oh, Jason, please. . . ."

"How can you bear to argue with me?" he asked harshly. "Cut it out."

14

The next day Jason made the necessary arrangements and drove Helen to a sanitorium 60 miles away. It was now up to her, he told her. She cried bitterly. He would come to see her every weekend, he said. Parting was painful. He couldn't understand why he felt like a nobody. But the whole core of his life had been in his concern for Helen, a very small worried life, he told himself, a man kidding himself day by day. On the drive home he began to suffer from a chilling numbness that bothered him. Turning on the car radio he listened intently as if waiting for a special announcement.

But when he went on duty that night, having had little sleep, he was more aloof and magisterial than ever. He was in an unmarked car downtown with his friend, Ira Mustard. It was raining. Ira was a big, jovial, happy, family man who went to church and had two children. Jason had often wished that Helen could have been friendly with May Mustard. But May was a loud, happy, vulgar woman who had never read a book.

Around midnight, it was still raining steadily, and Jason and Ira, patrolling their downtown beat, were talking amiably about the merits, from a spectator's view, of football and baseball. Jason liked football. Ira preferred the slower pace of baseball with its contrasting spurts of excitement. Rain was streaming across the windshield. Jason, driving, had to watch the road carefully.

"If you were playing football, Jason, what position would you like to play?" Ira asked.

"Well, let's see. I think I'd like to be a middle linebacker."

"No glamor in that job."

"You see everything going on—Christ, why am I talking about this?"

"What's the matter?"

"It's raining, Ira."

In the rain, visibility was poor. When they were on lower University, the police call came: "Watch for an old blue sedan driven by two men, proceeding east. A restaurant on Dundas has been robbed. These men are armed."

Two minutes later Ira said: "Look at that car, Jason, an old blue sedan." The car, coming up behind, passed them. In the heavy rain they caught only a glimpse of one of its occupants. As the car swerved erratically, Jason tried to catch up; he was a hundred feet behind. At the intersection there was an orange light. The other car, speeding up, got across the intersection and Jason, crossing against the red light, had to slow down. Ira said, "Take it easy just yet, Jason. Maybe it's just two drunken kids." So Jason stopped. But when he got the light he put his foot down heavily on the gas. The rain was so heavy he could hardly see the red taillight ahead, moving out near the center line as if the driver wanted to give himself lots of room. Jason came up on the inside lane. Just for a moment his window was opposite the other car's front window. Turning on his interior car light, and lowering his own window, Jason waved authoritatively. A man lowered his window too. Jason shouted, "Police. Pull over!" But the rain streamed in on him. Maybe in the rain Jason and Ira couldn't be recognized as policemen. The other window was raised hastily. Thrusting his arm out Jason yelled, "Stop. We're police! Police!" He forgot that in the rain his unmarked car could not be recognized as a police car. The other car raced on ahead. Outraged, Jason cursed softly.

"Take it easy, Jason," Ira said. "We'll get them at the next light." At the next light, College, they caught the car again, still on the inside lane. Jason lowered his window. "Police," he shouted. A young man, lowering his window, cupped his hand over his mouth, grinning crazily, shouting words that were lost; only ". . . you motherfucker," was clear, and there was a derisive gesture. At the intersection the cars had the green light. Then, in the middle of the intersecting street, the driver of the old car stopped suddenly, letting Jason shoot ahead across the road. As the old car wheeled behind them, swinging east, Jason imagined he heard wild laughter; he could almost see the big successful, contemptuous grins on the faces of the two men. "Well, that's them," he said to Ira. "No doubt about it now, Ira," and Ira said, "Yeah, and they're either smart or crazy. Probably doped up."

Jason tried to go into reverse and shoot back to the road. A car coming west in the rain, honking loud, had to swerve erratically, spraying water against the side of the car. "Wait. Another one," Ira said. Finally the road was clear, but when Jason made the turn, the red taillight was two blocks ahead of them; now it was just a glowing pinpoint. "The bastard. The little arrogant bastard," Jason said, but, trembling with excitement, he felt he was close to some deep satisfaction he needed. At the first red light, hardly slowing down, he swung the car crazily in front of an upcoming bus, bringing Ira trembling against him. Ira's hat fell off. "Jesus Christ, Jason," he gasped. "I've got a wife. Children."

Closing in on the red taillight, they passed the Gardens, then wide Jarvis street where they got the green light, and then they were in the old roominghouse district of dilapidated houses. The taillight suddenly vanished. "It turned in here," Ira said. "No, it turned the corner," Jason said. "In this Goddamned rain it could be just one of those cars parked at the curb," Ira said. "I say it went down Berkley," Jason insisted, refusing to slow down and let Ira see if anyone was in the row of parked cars. Berkley was a narrow, old, shabby street, poorly lighted and deserted. Far down this street they saw a taillight turning slowly left into a drive. "This is it, Ira," Jason yelled.

When Jason jumped out of the car he drew his gun. Ira had

his hand on his gun, but he did not draw it from the holster. In the rain they could hardly tell where they were. Not a light around. An open space, a wide, rutted cinder space, the ruts now full of water, in front of a low, sprawling, old building. Ira flashed his light on the building. It had a battered old sign, "Garage." The doors were closed. To the left on the cinder space, cars were parked side by side over as far as a falling down unpainted fence. Ira swung the flashlight around these cars. Through the sheet of rain in the corner by the fence in the garage was a car with the door open. There it was, the old blue car. Two men got out of the front seat. A door Jason could not see was slammed; the man who had used this door came around and stood with the other one. They were hatless, and in flashlit rain they stood startled, blinking their eyes. Then they came a little closer and stopped ten feet behind two old barrels. One of the barrels had fallen over.

"Alright, hands over your heads," Jason shouted. In the flashlight one of the men looked to be in his twenties, the other, who was slimmer, about seventeen. They had long hair, leather jackets shining wet, and open shirts. In that light their skins were brown or yellow.

"What is this?" the bigger one shouted belligerently. "Are you crazy?"

"Come forward, your hands up."

"Hey, cop, it's our car."

"Shut up. Step forward."

"What have we done?" the older one shouted. "What do you want to do?" He had an accent. "Give us a ticket? Okay," and he laughed. Then coming forward, boldly and arrogantly, threateningly sure of himself, he shoved his hand into an inside pocket of his jacket and pulled out something. A blinding flash in his own head made Jason shiver, as the man, hit on the chest, spun round, then came lurching forward over the barrel, rolling slowly to one side, his face in a puddle, a gurgling sound escaping from his gaping mouth. A little wail came from the smaller man, then a whimpering that seemed to come out of the sheets of rain. In Ira's flashlight this one's face was all screwed up like a bewildered child's. "You shot my

116

brother—my brother," he cried. Bawling, he threw himself on his brother's body.

Moving closer, his step slow, cautious, Ira put the flashlight on their heads, on their shiny hair and wet necks. Jason couldn't move. An extraordinary quiver within him stunned him. In his head at first and then through his whole body had been that blinding flash that seemed to push him in an anguished tension to the edge of an abyss, then hurl him over, but in the falling darkness the abyss opened up like a brilliant flower, and he had a blinding ecstatic awareness of the reality of himself, his life and all things that were exalting in this new awareness. It was the biggest thing he had ever had in his life; it was the biggest thing of all. He hardly heard Ira say: "Jason, I think he's dead."

"Ah—"

"Jason, for God's sake."

The younger brother, rising slowly, shrieked, "You killed Juan. Oh, you son of a bitch. Juan was only getting his driver's license. Look. It's there in his hand. Look at it."

The fallen driver's license lay half submerged in a little puddle. Yet it was there; and the brother's yelling was there too with the rain and the dead one, and lights coming on in the roominghouses, and Ira trying to restrain the brother. "Jason, get an ambulance. For God's sake, come out of it, Jason," Ira shouted.

"Oh, yeah. An ambulance," Jason said, and running to the car he called the ambulance. He also called in to the inspector and told what had happened. Then, standing on the lane, he felt exhausted. He liked the feel of the rain. He didn't want to think of anything or do anything, yet he had to rejoin Ira. He could hear the boy sobbing. Lights had come on in the old houses on both sides of the garage. Suddenly elderly men and women in old dressing gowns and with umbrellas came close, circling around. Soon there were many umbrellas in front of the garage. They were a black blanket widening under the flashing red ambulance light that was approaching. Ira shouted, "Come on, break it up. Go home. Get out of here."

Two more police cars came, the headlights from the three

117

cars lighting brightly part of the street and the stoops of the houses where people stood keeping out of the rain. Two solid detectives and Inspector Moffat, an older, quiet man, came toward the circle of umbrellas. Ira talked to him. The ambulance men had Juan, who as yet had no other name, on a stretcher, a sheet over his face. They lifted him up, and when they closed the door the sound the closing made was very abrupt.

"Alright, that's all," Ira said to the faces under the umbrellas. Jason looked around as if someone else was still speaking. Two plainclothesmen took the brother in their car to police headquarters, and Jason and Ira followed in their own car. Ira, who had picked up the driver's license, looked at it under his flashlight. "Juan Gonzalez."

"Spanish, maybe."

"Looked more like mulattos."

"Yeah," answered Jason and then nervously. "You saw the thing, Ira."

"Yeah."

"You saw him come at me."

"Sure I did."

"You saw what he did."

"You saw something, Jason. You must have—only what you saw wasn't there, was it?"

"You said they'd have guns, Ira."

"I know I did, Jason," Ira said and they had a sympathetic understanding. Police headquarters was only five minutes away. Mallory, the duty inspector, had already got the story from Inspector Moffat. "Pretty rough, Dunsford," he said to Jason. He knew Jason was a man who could hold his temper. "There's the other one. Seems to be in shock." The brother, soaking wet and shaking, his eyes glazed, all the fight gone out of him, was slumped on a chair. He had been searched; he had identification cards indicating that Gonzalez was his name. He was from Panama, he said. He had been in the country six years, living with his mother, who didn't speak very good English. She was a cleaning woman, working in downtown

118

offices at night. Restaurants? Robbing? He didn't know anything about robbing restaurants. He and his brother had been at a party and had a few drinks; ten fellows and girls were at the party. Inspector Mallory asked him where the party had been. He gave the address dully. "Yeah, it's in the phone book. I think. I remember my brother called." Muddled and broken as he was, he remembered names of people who had been at the party and told where some of them lived. A detective immediately got a phone book and telephoned the address of the house. In a few moments he rejoined them. "That was the wife of someone," the detective said. "The boy and his brother were there all evening. Lots of witnesses. They must be in the clear. I guess that's it." Only then did Tony Gonzalez, groping apologetically, very scared now, stand up. "What about Juan?" he asked. "Juan is dead. What do I say to my mother when she comes home? How do I tell this when she say, Why?"

"It's tough, son. But there is an explanation," Inspector Mallory said gruffly. "When the police say stop, you stop. You don't run. This is terrible for you, I know. I'm sorry. Someone will drive you home and stay with you and talk to your mother." And the boy was taken away.

"This is one hell of a mess, Jason," Mallory said. "Come on into the office. We'll make out a report and go over this. Wait, I'll put in a few phone calls. I don't want the press to hear about this immediately. Thank God, he's a Panamanian. Not enough of them around to make trouble. Thank God." Jason, who had said little, impressed them all with his dignified, unprotesting air of solitude. One part of his mind was painfully aware, grieving with the dead brother. He could see him going home, see him flopping down, getting up, trembling, crying, dreading the return of his mother. But the other part of Jason's mind held him apart, kept him untouched, gave him his strange wondering stillness.

"Dunsford, Dunsford, do you hear me? We've got to get a statement, and you too, Mustard," said the inspector, who had returned from making his telephone calls. "The chief is out somewhere speaking at a banquet. The deputy chief is coming down here. I'm trying to touch all the bases. I've asked Gotlieb to come down. We may need a lawyer like Gotlieb."

The deputy chief, Marlow, a tall, thin, very loyal man, came in. He already knew the story. Jason talked, then Ira talked. "I'll tell you one thing, sir," Ira said. "No one wanted to be violent: I've never seen a man as shocked as Dunsford after he fired and the suspect's hand came out of his pocket with no gun in it. He was frozen in surprise, sir. Maybe the suspect was only being a showoff, sir. But Officer Dunsford was stunned stiff, so sure was he that the suspect was pulling a gun on him."

Turning to Jason who even now seemed off by himself, he said, "Take it easy, Jason."

When Gotlieb arrived he sat down with them and had them go over and over the story. He got at the important little details; in the car chase the men had shouted obscenities; that was important. How close had the dead man come, making the threatening gesture? A threatening step, then the hand going suddenly into the pocket? Close? Closer than that? Even closer? Yes. A sound story. Slumping back in the chair, Gotlieb brooded. It would be his suggestion to the chief and the police commission, he said finally, that Jason should not be suspended. A suspension might suggest that his conduct was open to question. It would suggest that there should be a public inquiry. No, he thought, if it was possible, there should be an inquest rather than an inquiry, under the direction of a coroner to determine simply how the man died and by whose hand and whether it was an accidental death. With luck, that would be the end of it.

They asked Jason to wait outside while they deliberated further.

In the corridor Jason, pacing up and down, couldn't take his eyes off the new shiny tiled floor. Jason had great faith in the plump, shrewd Gotlieb. A fund raiser who might become the next attorney general. A cleaning woman was mopping the tiles. Plump and gray with a tired pale face, she never looked up from her work, coming closer to Jason in his pacing. Suddenly he was acutely aware of her. He began to take great care not to step on her clean spots on the floor. Yet she wouldn't look up at him; he was just feet and legs to her. While he waited to be gripped by some terrible remorse, a lot seemed to depend on whether she would put her eyes on him. One steady, wandering glance from the stooped cleaning woman might have demoralized him. It might have reminded him of his mother whom he had respected and admired. But the cleaning woman wouldn't raise her head. He was to be left alone suffering some terrible remorse. Then suddenly he didn't mind being alone. It was really surprising; he could let himself be, feel his whole being filling again with that exalted, stunning sense of his own enlargement, that exhilarating sense of himself being hurled into the center of things which he had felt standing in the rain after the gun went off.

"Dunsford," Inspector Mallory called, opening the office door.

"Yes sir?"

"You can go home if you want to or finish your shift with Mustard."

"I'll go with Mustard, sir."

"Good man."

The following morning a picture of Jason appeared in the paper, a good picture of a handsome, smiling, friendly cop, taken five years ago, just after Jason had heard that his wife was pregnant and before her miscarriage. He had been proud and happy. The story accompanying the picture was a sympathetic account of what had happened. Officer Dunsford had not been suspended; there would be an inquest to determine how Juan Gonzalez had died, especially since he had been cleared of any involvement in that particular robbery. The badly frightened mother of the boys had shrieked at the reporter, "Justice! Justice! Where is the justice? Where is my good boy?"

15

Jason's picture in the morning paper was on the kitchen table, right under Lisa's eyes as she sipped her coffee. She was late for work again, not getting enough sleep lately. It wasn't until later, after they had been to a movie with Jake and Wilma Fulton and were going into the Park Plaza for a drink that Al said: "Let's see what's going on in the world; I haven't seen a paper all day." He bought a newspaper.

They went up to the roof bar, but it was too chilly on the terrace, and the lounge was crowded. The tall, lovely Helena bowed to them and smiled to herself. Jake liked coming to these bars with his handsome Wilma. His air of authority reassured everyone who looked at him. Through these bar contacts made with his flowing scholarly ease, Jake had got himself on three television talk shows. He also liked ordering the drinks.

Al read the newspaper, and Lisa turned to Wilma to tell her how much she liked her new hairdo. It made her look like a bold, Icelandic pirate princess, she said. Wilma and Jake, as man and wife, fascinated Lisa. They were always together, yet they seemed able to do without each other. They had real brawls, too. Once Jake had slapped her, and once she had tried to club him with the heel of her shoe. Yet they laughed a lot when they were together. Wilma, whose father was a rich doctor, had grown up with three brothers and three sisters and had her own kind of big family emotional security. The only thing Lisa had against her was that she couldn't buy a dress without Wilma inquiring where she had got it, and if she had paid the full price; then Wilma would go to the boutique and ask for the same dress at the same price.

"Well, for God's sake," Al said. "Look—it's my cop."

"Your *cop*?" Jake said.

"You know, the one who grabbed Shore."

"What's he done now?"

"Shot a kid. Killed a kid."

"Oh no. Let's see."

They passed the paper around.

"This is uncanny," Al said. "I think Shore just looking at that cop could tell he was full of violence."

"You couldn't tell by this picture," Lisa said.

"It doesn't look like him. The expression's all wrong."

"I'm sure it is," Jake said cynically. "They have cop-shots for all occasions: 'Your happy, smiling, friendly, neighborhood cop.'"

"The thing is," Al said, "Shore had this guy taped. You should have heard Shore talk to him."

"What did he say?"

"You'd have sworn he knew the cop had it in for him."

"Cut it out, Al."

"I was there, wasn't I? I remember the way that cop's face came looming into the light. It was so full of sullen discontent. I wonder if Shore's in town?"

"Give him a call."

"Maybe I will."

"Shore's the head office, isn't he?"

"That's what I like about you, Jake. You always know the exact value of things."

Jake smiled helplessly, then opened his hands toward Al and said: "So now my values are all wrong."

Al was taken aback. With that big smile, Jake seemed to be

confessing some kind of failure, and Al grew embarrassed. He got up, saying, "Yeah, I'll phone,"

"Al's changed," Lisa said, watching him leave. "Don't you think he's changed, Jake?"

"Sure—and it's great."

"Great?"

"He's got something going for him."

"Is it so great, though?"

"If he gets down to it."

"But he's *not* getting down to it. Shore was no help."

"It doesn't matter. I don't know what he's after, but he'll come up with something good. He makes me feel, well, that all my hopes are in my sidelines; Man's hope—his sidelines, his moonlighting. That's what the moon means in our time: a job on the side. How about that?" He laughed.

"Al's all wound up, and he's better-looking for it," Wilma said.

"Wilma likes her men to be wound up before they get to her."

"Why not?" Wilma said. "Let something else do it to them before they get to me. I'm lazy."

Jake had always been able to assume the heavy authority of a compassionate bishop. He knew it was a good tone. He knew it made him a good teacher, even on his bad days when he actually had very little to say, because a good teacher was a good actor. Now, both his hands came out, big open hands. Wanting to offer some consoling help, he meant what he said, believing that he was right about Al. "Look, Lisa," he said, "The trouble is that Eugene Shore is alive. He's here breathing down Al's neck. Al can't talk about Shore with any finality. But if Shore were dead. . . ."

"Why do they have to be dead?"

"They all look different the day after they die. A little time passes, then suddenly you see them in perspective. That's why I had no trouble with Fitzgerald. But with Shore right here in town. . . ."

"You're awful," Lisa said. "Morticians. That's what you all

125

are. Morticians." But Jake went on talking about the relation-ship between the artist and the scholar. Lisa began to resent not only his authority but the way he now seemed to be conducting a seminar, carried away by his own "wisdom."

"How many phone calls is Al making?" she said restlessly. "Order me another drink, Jake; I'll get Al."

Al was by himself at the parapet, looking out over the city. The upper part of his body was outlined against the night sky. He looked as he had the night he stood at the rim of the Campidoglio Square in Rome, staring down at the Forum, only much bigger now. By the set of his head and fixed stare she knew he wasn't seeing orderly patterns of lights stretching for miles. Was he seeing alleys in the rain, a garage and the blast of a gun, the gun's flash becoming another one of those lights? Turning to her as she joined him, he pointed. "Those boys lived somewhere over there." He let his eyes sweep around. "Our town, no great crimes. No great tombs. No history." In the sky to the west was a sudden fiery glow, widening, then bright-ening, then shadowed, then the bursting glow again. "A big fire," he said. "The chances are it's a lumberyard. Our dawn light."

"Did you talk to Shore?"

"He wasn't in."

"Is it all that important?"

"To me. I suppose so."

"Come on, let's have our drink and go home. I'm really awfully tired."

"My little darling," he said, his arm around her as they went back to the table, "Why do you never look tired? Alright, let's go home. Listen, let's clip out that story and send it to Shore in case he missed it. I'm going to ask him to go to the inquest with me. I'm sure he'd like to be there. Wouldn't you say so?"

"I don't know," she began, then, glancing at him she cried out within herself, "Oh, Goddamn that stupid cop," for she had caught the glint in Al's eye, the glint she knew came from his expectation of finding in Shore's concern for someone she was willing to believe was just a ruthless cop—yet another vista.

16

During the next few days she couldn't help wanting to be with Al all the time, she liked so much his new happy ease with himself. He was full of new impulses that charmed her, and she liked his sudden moments of wondering gentleness. His restless fancies made her feel they were excitingly close to something good for them right there in town. But these feelings she found so hard to control began to bewilder her. She felt irresponsible, for she could see that his work habits hadn't changed at all, nor had they in the direction he was going. Meeting Shore had only heightened his desire to have the work go on and on and on, and now he was imagining new stuff would be coming in on Shore and the cop. What is Al now, she asked herself, worrying. A life-starved, love-starved professor? No, whatever else he was, he wasn't love-starved. Al was a lover, but now he was in love with a vision. Then, feeling stricken, she asked herself, "What about his job? How is he going to live? What about me?"

Late at night he still went out alone, and when he came in she would listen for his familiar movements as he changed into his working clothes. She had made a mistake. She had blurted out impatiently: "For God's sake, Al, don't you want to see it finished? So you can turn to something else? So you can be your own man again?" He had looked at her for a long time, full of wondering surprise, then sudden resentment. "You forget things," he said. "I could say a thing or two, but I won't." She pretended to herself that she didn't know what he meant, and after that night, if he was out very late, he did not come into the bedroom when he returned, and tonight she was in bed, waiting and feeling lonely.

Her eyes were accustomed to the darkness. She could see the shadows fading on the ceiling and a thin light touching the dresser against the wall. In this kind of darkness when Al used to come in, he would reach for her thigh. "What's Peggy got to say tonight?" Why did he call it Peggy? And then suddenly while she nursed this mixture of loneliness and resentment, Shore began to loom in her mind. She could see him clearly, self-centered, powerful, always having his own way. Shore's law! A human being, yes. Yes, he was. And big and tall as he might be in his own secretly wild humanity, he would be flattered to know that he had created a world which one young man could enter, then believe he must never leave it, a world without end. How gratifying to an artist. In his great pride Shore would go on being charmingly elusive with Al. Why shouldn't he? He was human. Had anyone else ever made him feel so big? But you and I know each other, Mr. Shore, she thought grimly, and in her fancy she began to play with him. She put his beaver hat on his head and there he was on the City Hall steps in the noon sunlight and there was a crowd and dignitaries and the mayor. They were in a circle around him, and he was wearing his double-breasted suit. Three clergymen stood behind the mayor, who was stroking his toothbrush moustache. The mayor was smiling. "Sir, you sir," the mayor said, "you are a law-abiding citizen, but your work is subversive in the worst way. There's a lot of fraud and rottenness and criminality in people, but sir, the tablets on which your work is written have to be destroyed. Sir, we weep for you, but you must go. You must leave this city." Mr. Shore took off his beaver hat, stroked it, and then put it on the mayor's head and began to go, miles away, miles and miles away, smiling his little bemused smile, the figure getting smaller, fading, then vanishing. Gone, gone.

Suddenly Lisa sat up in bed, coldly certain that Al would never finish his work on Shore, his whole future in heaps of notes and midnight walks. She bowed her head over her hunched-up knees. Then she got out of bed, and stiff and alert, stood in the dark saying aloud, "But the work is done. It's done." She went to his room.

He had left the light on. She knew that everything she had typed was in the top drawer of the desk. While taking it out she saw his journal open on the desk. He had written: "I'm absorbed in this new exciting approach. But it struck me today—Why should a work ever be finished? While a thing is unfinished, it is alive. That is exciting. Einstein said his theories were unfinished. Maybe I know this intuitively. Yet in all this, where is Lisa? Do I still look too hard at things? . . ."

Lisa's surge of protective sympathy shattered her. She slumped over the desk, her head on her arms, and then all her natural generosity was aroused.

She studied his manuscript, reading the pages carefully, and then all his notes. She sat back for a moment, elated by a sudden sense of distance from the material; this was always how she was at her best at work, when, with that curious sense of removal you found that you were more in touch with the shape, the outline, the way a thing should be organized. It was all there. She could see it, and Al's comments and sharp little asides, these were what brought it alive. She would fit them into the general outline. It was good. It was her kind of work, and she went at it feverishly. More than an hour later she heard the sound of the latch, and she hurried to bed, pretending to be asleep. He stayed in the kitchen. She listened for the smallest comforting movements: his step, the moving of the kettle on the stove, his sitting down and opening the morning newspaper, and she knew he was all right, and lay back, trembling with relief.

The next evening, while he was out walking alone in the streets, she worked, shaping what she was sure was the crux of his view of Shore's work. She did the same the next night, and at the office, on the third day, she typed through her lunch hour and all that afternoon. Her boss looked quizzically at her once or twice, but she had no trouble from him. He was putty in her hands.

17

When Lisa came home, Al had dinner ready. He was wearing his striped sweater, standing at the stove. "For heaven's sake, Al, sit down," she pleaded. "Let me do it." Seeing how upset she was, he sat down with baffled amusement. They ate. He went to his room, and when she had done the dishes she took the 20-page outline from her bag and went to him.

He was at his desk, leaning back in the chair, some penciled notes in his hand, and he didn't look in the least unhappy.

"Hey, Al," she said brightly.

"What?"

"How would you like to meet a great editor?"

"Where do we have to go?"

"To an old friend—Lisa."

"You? You mean they've given you another job?"

Very diffidently, she said, "Now don't jump down my throat. Just listen. I found all that stuff I typed going round and round in my head, and it seemed to have a pattern. I just had to show how, for me anyway, it all came together. So here's the outline. Will you look at it?"

"Why sure," he said smiling and taking her manuscript.

He was looking at it with genuine curiosity and surprise, then settled down, read steadily, and finally leaned back, meditating with the manuscript on his knee. Half to himself, he said: "Looking back on it like this is interesting, really interesting." Then his tone changed. "This is a very competent job, Lisa."

"Well, at least it's all there—I think." she said, trying to hide her relief.

"It's wonderful. Why did you do it?"

"On a hunch. Is it helpful? Can you use it?"

"Use it?" he asked, and he stared at her, wondering and embarrassed. "No, Lisa, I can't."

"Why not?"

"Because it's the old stuff, just put in shape."

"But maybe that's all that was needed."

"Come on Lisa. Do you think I've been sweating through these last few weeks just because I needed a carpenter?"

"A *carpenter,*" she cried, stung. "Excuse me." The hurt to her pride, mixed with her despairing concern, bewildered her. "Goddamn it," she blurted out. "I'm only thinking of your career. Time passes; nothing gets done. What about your career?"

"Career," he said, holding up the manuscript as he laughed. "You don't understand, Lisa. I've gone beyond this."

"Gone beyond! To what? The woodwork's crawling with hungry little Ph.D.'s. Every busboy has a Ph.D."

"Shut up."

"I won't shut up."

"Then I'll shut you up."

"Try it."

He got up, and the outraged hardness in his eyes, so unfamiliar to her, made her want to cry out desperately, Why don't you need me now? but she lost her head. "Who in the hell do you think you are?" she said fiercely. "What was your big day this week? A cop gets his picture in the papers. It made your day. Stuff I wrap the garbage in before I throw it out. You're an expert on crimes that aren't crimes. Criminals that aren't criminals. Cops that aren't cops. Shore's riffraff."

"Tell that one to Chekhov," he shouted.

"Chekhov?" she said with outraged scorn. "I wouldn't need to tell Chekhov a thing. He'd understand perfectly the real crime here."

"What crime?"

"What you do to me around here."

"It's your place. Call the cop. Have me thrown out." Then he faltered, stricken as she confronted him, her jaw set. She felt his eyes emptying of her. It was a strange feeling.

"You just can't hold anything back," he said, his voice breaking. "It all has to come out. It seems like a warm and love-ly thing. It makes people go your way, go where they don't want to go. Why not? You always pay the shot. You can afford to give up people, things, if they don't measure up to your warmth. College. The arts school. Those guys you loved a little. What made me look at you and think that we—" Shaking his head, he cried desperately, "What are you, anyway?"

"Your rubber ball."

"Yeah, well where're you going to bounce to now?"

"Right over your head, like you weren't even there." But her own humiliation became unbearable, and she screamed. "How can you see anything, you bone-picking scholar? How can you know about anything that's alive?" Fierce with the fullness of herself, she went a step closer.

"For God's sake," he cried, raising his arm protectively. "Get off me. I've seen enough." Confused by what he had said, he shouted, "Of course it's a crime, my being here. You're damned right," and he grabbed his jacket on the couch and fled.

She heard him trip on the stairs and thought he had fallen, but then the front door slammed. She stood at the head of the stairs, confused because the good she had wanted for him had hurt him painfully. Yet he was outrageous! Day by day he had grown more outrageous. Now he would be sitting in the park, coming alive under the pain of his wounded vanity. It was all his selfish sense of himself, she thought angrily, yet she hurried for her coat. At the door, pale, pretty, young Mrs. Atlee, whose

133

husband, a geophysicist, stayed out all night, saying he snatched a little sleep in his lab, spoke to Lisa. "Mr. Delaney was in an awful hurry, wasn't he? I thought he fell on the stairs." Lisa said easily, "We were late. I kept him late. I keep everybody late. He had to hurry. You know how it is, Mrs. Atlee, when you keep a man waiting."

In the park, children were playing. The street lights came on. Older boys grouped around a bench teased two girls their own age who giggled as they complained. Near the fountain a kid, his mouth full of water, squirted it at a passing girl. Mothers were coming out to get their children and take them home.

Lisa decided to go back home and take a hot bath to soothe her nerves. Nothing seemed as complicated when she was lying in the tub, the warm water as high as her chin, and for an hour, lying in the bath, she soothed herself, but when she got up to put on a robe she couldn't bear to look at the bed which was suddenly the one dark lonely place. Hours passed. She thought of Jake Fulton. She called him. In an easy casual tone she asked if Al were there with him. No. Well, it wasn't important. Al could call if he dropped in. She had a message for him. But while she joked with Jake, her own fraudulent brightness told her suddenly that Al's nerves were shattered. In a trance somewhere, he wouldn't know which way to turn. So she said goodbye and sat and waited for the phone to ring. Holding onto Al in her thoughts, she kept her whole being suffused with the warmth of the protective sympathy that was so necessary to her nature. When she went to bed she couldn't sleep. A faint streak of light on the bedroom ceiling kept shifting; she heard the familiar little night sounds. A night bird startled her. A cat screeched, and the screech seemed to tear out a part of her good life with Al. A feeling she dreaded, having experienced it before, began to depress her; a sudden disbelief in everything. By morning, if the feeling grew, she would again be nursing her old boredom. This boredom had been complete misery, a real suffering. Her knowledge of her own nature frightened her. Unless she could love someone with all the fullness of her being, she became ruthless and destructive. And now, telling

134

herself Al had gone for good, and feeling emptied, she wished she could believe in something outside her own life. She wished she could be a Marxist or a Calvinist or a Catholic. But the people she knew who had these fantasies had always bored her. As she remembered it, her father in his youth had been a Catholic. A speculator, a gambler, he would remain superstitious until his death. Now, in the dark of night, wherever her father was, he would have something to turn to, yet she had only this hunger gnawing within her. Suddenly she got out of bed in alarm. Al might not have his key. Hurrying to his room, she searched all his pockets, his other jacket, his good, dark suit, then she felt weak with relief. He must have the key with him.

Four days passed. At the office no one could tell that beautiful Lisa Tolen had had a man walk out on her. Her vivid, lipsticked, wide mouth remained set in a warm smile. After work she began to go across the road with the girls to have a beer instead of hurrying home. She dreaded the empty apartment. There her mind would be full of little homely scenes; sitting in the kitchen with Al having a cup of coffee; or loafing along window-shopping with him; the way he wore his striped sweater at work; the night she had insisted on trimming his spade beard. Yet she had to be at home. He might call. All alone, waiting for the phone to ring, she grew more apprehensive and decided to go downstairs and ask Mrs. Atlee to come up and have a drink with her. But on the stairs she felt ashamed. Mrs. Atlee, who was tormented, never knowing when her husband would come home, had told her that three other wives on the street were abandoned by their husbands and they often had drinks together; a street club; women with something in common. At the window again, Lisa looked out. It was a good quiet street. Nothing wrong with the street, only the women who lived on it. Then she spent an hour calling girls she had liked in college, girls who had married well; they all cried, "Lisa, is it you? Where have you been?" and she chattered enthusiastically about joining ballet committees and working for the Cancer Society. By midnight, when there was no one else to call and she was sitting by the phone, she seemed to know where Al was. She could see him in a little room, sitting on the bed, heavily depressed, only leaving the room to buy a quart of milk and cans of soup. He hadn't shaved. If there was a knock on the door he wouldn't answer. In a rage of concern for him she collapsed on the couch and slept.

18

Jake called the next evening. He said reassuringly, "It's alright, Lisa. I've heard from Al."

"Then you know. . . ."

"Yes, he told me."

"Is he alright?"

"Yes, he says he's alright."

"Where is he?"

"He wouldn't tell me."

"Jake—then why are you calling me?"

"Al was worried about you. Are you alright, Lisa?"

"Am I alright? What is this? Oh, poor Al," and she was alarmed. "Why are you calling? What's happening to Al?"

"The fact is, he sounds quite alright," Jake insisted. Then, with his impulsive sympathy, he said, "Are you alone? Come out and have a drink."

"Good God, Jake, I'm not hysterical."

"I know you're not. But sitting around is no good." Then he said impishly, "How about a game of pool?" Jake, his wife, and Al and Lisa had often played pool together. But it struck her now that Jake was trying to break some bad news to her, trying to make it easy. She was certain Al was in trouble somewhere. "Gladly," she said. "Maybe a game of pool is just what I need." She would meet him in an hour.

The pool parlor on Yonge Street, a new, antiseptic place catering to women as well as men, had pink broadloom on the floor and the pyramids of light over the green tables made them look like exotic palms on a big pink flower. Young women were at the tables; over the clicking of the billiard balls she could hear the little cries of pleasure from the women. Even now Lisa looked around, as she always did, to make sure that she was more elegant than any other woman there.

Jake's conservative tweed jacket and tie and his warm, dark face and big shoulders comforted her. Already she felt closer to Al. Jake's clothes consoled her, too. He would never work, day after day, in the same striped sweater. Yet from the beginning she was aware of Jake keeping his eye on her. It bothered her. She waited apprehensively, trying to mock him with a mysterious smile, offering a small bet on the first game. She kept moving competently around the table, lining up her shots, but then, suddenly, turning on him, she banged the heel of her cue imperiously on the floor, demanding, "What is this, Jake? Where's Al? Where is he?"

"My God, Lisa," he pleaded. "I said I didn't know."

"Didn't you ask him?"

"He doesn't want me to know."

"So I'm not to know. I see." In her bewilderment she had to walk away, hiding her pain. "Oh, this lousy male loyalty. It's disgusting," she said bitterly.

"Lisa—if Al thinks the answer to his problem is to be alone with his work, let him be. Stay out of it." With gentle concern in his dark face, his hand came out, but she knocked it away fiercely. "I don't need sympathy. Don't you dare patronize me, Jake Fulton." As he stiffened resentfully she saw that he really didn't know where Al was, and if he kept looking into her face she would cry.

"What are you going to do, Lisa?"

"Play a little pool with you, Jake."

"Well, watch me on this one."

138

"I was very good for Al, wasn't I, Jake?"

"Al knows how much he owes you."

"To lose out to another woman," she said with a little smile, "that's one thing. But to the work of a kindly, middle-aged man. My God."

"What?"

"Shore."

"You a loser?"

"I've always been a loser. I don't know why," she said, frowning as she watched her ball click gently against another one. "All my life, always about the biggest things. Didn't you know that, Jake?"

"When did you learn to play pool, Lisa?"

"Oh, years ago. Once when my father came to town, he spent the whole afternoon teaching me how to play pool. It was a peculiar way to spend your one day with your father."

"I think you could beat Al."

"I did beat him—in Paris."

"Did he like it?"

"No, he wanted to keep on playing."

"Al is very good." Jake was avoiding her eyes. He was a good friend. The honesty he might have put in his work he gave instead to his friends. Chalking his cue, he said, "Look Lisa. Al is a scholar. Do you know what that means?" He sounded bitter. "A man trained to try and think and feel and live in the mind of his subject, who happens, in this case, to be Eugene Shore, and it ties a man in knots." Then he sighed. "The awful thing is, it's the occupational hazard. A man can end up with no mind of his own at all."

She had put down her cue on a table. "I had a feeling I was coming out to meet Al. That you meant to take me to him. Now I have the feeling that he's in this neighborhood. Let's look around, Jake. Will you? Let's look in the Riverboat. He used to drop in there. Who's there now?"

"Oh, one more guitar picker from the suburban desert. A new girl," Jake said. He was glad to leave the poolroom and the bright lights. He could no longer hide how disturbed he was.

139

It was a mild night, and by the way he took her arm walking up the street, she knew he was as worried about Al as she was. "I'm not trying to upset you, Lisa. Please believe me," he said. "Yet I ask myself if Al really shouldn't be left alone. Oh, I mean it, Lisa." And then troubled and unhappy himself, "In a way, I envy him. We were two pretty competent guys, making our plans. Nothing we couldn't organize and handle. It goes back a long way with me. My father used to tell me that I should learn, above all things, to defend myself financially so I could hold to the secret things that were important to me. I'm so good at this now, Lisa, so damned good at defending myself that I sometimes forget what it is I'm supposed to be defending. Oh, I'm getting along. Things keep coming my way. I can handle all the smart bastards coming against me. But Al . . . now he's found something he can't organize, and Goddamn it, I envy him. What is it, Lisa? Something hidden from him? A way of looking at things? An effect in life? An effect in art that's wonderfully mysterious? Lisa, I have no sense of mystery at all. I know more than you about some things, and what it is, I think I know. Maybe having no sense of mystery means having no real sense of love, eh, Lisa?"

His hand tightening on her arm and drawing her closer only made her feel more lonely. At the intersection where they waited for the red light to change, Jake went on: "With everything looking different to Al now, maybe he looks at you and me, wishing we weren't so. . . ."

"Jake, what are you trying to tell me?"

"I don't know," and he tried to laugh. "I guess I'm in a ridiculous mood. Hey, look."

Passing the shops, they had come to Isaac's art gallery. In the doorway to the right of the gallery, in the dark doorway that led to a stairs, a young man of twenty, in a Hindu shirt and jeans, crouched on his haunches in the shadows; opposite him in this doorway, sitting cross-legged, was a young girl, her long hair swinging down over a notebook resting on her knee. The young man had a flute. He would play a few bars, and the girl would nod and write down the notes. The young man played

140

again, still just a few bars, waiting; the girl made the notations. So intent were they, so absorbed in this moment, that they didn't even notice Lisa and Jake.

"Al would like this," Jake said.

"Jake, I like it too," she insisted.

"Who said you didn't?"

"Well, the way you said it."

On their way to the Riverboat they were following Al in the walk he used to take when he wanted to hear the folksingers he liked. At this hour, because it was like a summer night, the street was crowded. Young people drifted slowly along the pavement; cars full of sedate gapers blocked the road. Moving slowly in the crowd, Jake and Lisa passed little boutiques in battered old houses and new expensive restaurants, and there, that most quixotic spot, the old folks home, where elderly people sat on lounging chairs watching the new life flow by. Some people in town were proud of this little neighborhood of hippies, junkies, and discontented, bored, high school girls. The people who were proud said the little neighborhood showed how the town was in close touch with the restless boredom of the outside world. Reaching the corner, Lisa and Jake stood looking aimlessly across the road at the bright opulent hotel, half expecting to see Al cross the road, having had his drink at the bar.

They sat on the patio of one of the new cafes, opposite the nightclub with the strobe lights, Danish movies, and naked dancing girls. They had bowls of onion soup and a half-bottle of wine, then more wine, until Lisa believed Al, out walking, would be drawn to this place. Why not? People had these sudden hunches. It was a good thing that life was full of these mysterious compulsions.

"Lisa, look," Jake said. "Don't they look like a couple of clowns?" Across the street, two well-dressed, middle-aged businessmen had just come out of the Danish movie parlor. They stood in the night street, in the midst of that drab lethargy, stunned and befuddled, and then with little furtive laughs they went on their way. "Stupefied, eh?" Jake said chuckling.

"The naked girls, the crotch shots still flashing in their minds. Not quite ready for their hotel and convention colleagues."

A pretty, plump, young girl in a yellow sweater came slowly and sedately along the street, close to Lisa. As she came into the light, her soft young face had all the serene security that came from knowing of a meeting ahead, the needed meeting; it was all in the yielding contentment of her face and her slow proud walk. Her eyes on the girl, Lisa said nervously, "Tell me something, Jake, why can't Al see that Mr. Shore is, after all, an ordinary man?"

"Come on now, Lisa. How can he be ordinary?"

"He's nice, he's noble, he's lordly, I know, Jake, but he has corrupted Al. Al has nothing to believe in now." Her head went back so arrogantly that two men at the next table gaped, then, held by her beauty, watched intently, waiting. "It's the ordinary stuff in Shore that Al won't face. The rotten human stuff," she protested.

"I don't know," Jake said, bemused as he looked at her closely. "No, I don't know what I'd do if a girl loved me as much as you love Al. No, I mightn't be able to take it." A sudden gust of wind blew scraps of paper along the street, driving them momentarily against their legs and then on down the street. The people on the street were all hurrying away. There was a low rumble. "Hear that?" Jake asked.

"A thunderstorm, I guess," she said.

"Let's get home. Come on," he said.

Lightning flashed across the sky as they got in the taxi. On the short drive to Lisa's place they were silent. Leaving her, Jake said, "I'll hear from Al. Don't worry, Lisa."

"And I won't?" she asked.

"He's not in love with me, Lisa."

"What?" she said, startled.

"I'll let you know. I swear it, Lisa. As soon as I hear from him."

"Good night, Jake," she said, kissing him impulsively. "You're a sweet man. I love you." She didn't look back, though she knew he was sitting in the taxi worrying, watching her go into the house.

On the dark stairs, pausing, she listened intently, then went on up, turned on the television set, and collapsed in an armchair. Thunder rattled and cracked. She waited for the sound of rain outside, the rain pouring down. She waited long past midnight for the rain, but it didn't come. Then it was time to try the darkness of the bedroom again. She put on her short nightie that hardly covered her navel, went into the bathroom, brushed her long hair, brushing and brushing while watching her face in the mirror. Then she took off the nightie, intending to take her hot bath. Instead, she got a can of beer from the refrigerator and sat morosely at the end of the kitchen table. Finishing the first can, she quickly opened another. She lined up the empty cans, and her nerves were soothed; within her was a wonderful bright stillness. Her elbow on the table, her hand holding back her long hair, she began to have the most satisfactory glowing perceptions about this place, her home. Poor dear Al! What a weakling he had become. Imagine inviting a man by the name of Eugene Shore into his house, an ordinary kind of guy who just smiled wisely and said nothing, and playing a dumb game with him, Al pretending he was a horse and the old boy on his back was Marcus Aurelius, and then Al had really begun to believe he was just a horse, and maybe not a good enough horse for the emperor, and there they were now, playing in her living room, lurching around, grown men turning her house into a playpen.

Getting up, Lisa moved majestically into the bedroom, fell on the bed, rolled over on her back, and slept.

At the office the next afternoon she had a hunch about Mr. Shore. He liked her very much; of that she was quite sure; she could always tell. She telephoned, and when Mr. Shore answered, she said, "Oh, Mr. Shore, I'm really sorry about this. But I know you feel involved." Her voice broke. She caught her breath sharply, then let the words pour out. "You know the state Al was in; well, he blew up. Yes, he did. God knows what he's apt to do now. Maybe he's holed up somewhere, depressed or not eating, and you're so terribly involved in this. I can't get near him. I don't know where he is. Can I see you, Mr. Shore?" The long silence frightened her. "Lisa," Mr. Shore said finally. The sound of his voice, so calm and friendly, soothed her. "Of course you can see me. I'll be in this evening."

Just after nine, with the street lights lit, the ravine was a great gully of moving shadows. Lisa parked her car just down the street and came hurrying to the house in her brown suede skirt and yellow sweater with an air of embarrassed dignity, and the house now, after the weeks that had passed, was covered with ivy. Mr. Shore answered the door.

19

He had on a fawn-colored jacket, just like the marvelous jacket Lisa had thought of buying for Al. This astonished her and she drew back uneasily. But he was leading her into his living room, sitting her in the couch by the window, and she had no time to look around. As he stood solidly in front of her in the jacket that would have looked much better on Al, she felt the room's warmth.

"Lisa, I'm sure Al's alright," he said. "The tantrum of an overworked man. The help you offered was all too generous, too wonderfully concerned. He'll see it."

"I just wish Al could hear you." she said. Then reflecting, frowning, silent for a moment, she looked up. "I know I am doing a terrible thing that could only end in a dreadful humiliation. I was desperate. I'm really half out of my mind right now." Fumbling in her purse, she took out a slip of paper and handed it to him. "This is the phone number of Al's friend, Fulton. He'll be hearing from Al. I wondered if you could call Fulton and ask him to tell Al you want to see him. Al will get in touch with you. I'm sure of it." Shore still said nothing. "Is there anything wrong with this?" she asked nervously.

"Well, first I think we should have a drink," he said, glancing dubiously at the slip of paper. "Nothing looks as alarming after a good drink."

"I could do with a drink," she said, sighing.

"So could I. What'll you have, Lisa?"

"A gin and tonic would be nice. I don't drink much, you know."

"I'll have brandy myself," he said. A big brass tray was on the oak table at the end of the room under a Chagall. He had put bottles there and an ice bucket and some glasses. With his back to her, he poured the drinks with unruffled ease.

"I like your pictures, Mr. Shore," she said vaguely.

"Do you like painting?" he asked without turning.

"I don't like Chagall."

"Well, it's a small one."

"I could never bring myself to like Chagall. Too folksy, too quaint."

"A free imagination. That's the thing. The only thing, Lisa," he said as he came to her with the drinks. The lack of sympathy in his face shocked her. "I can't be a go-between," he said firmly. "It's something between you and Al."

"Oh, I'm sorry. I'm so sorry, Mr. Shore."

"It's alright, Lisa. You see, I don't know what goes on between you two. Nor should I know. Those are the intimate things."

"Intimate?" she said, her eyebrows going up. "This has nothing to do with intimate things, Mr. Shore."

"I think you'll find it has."

"No, it's other things. It's this one tragic thing. Al's a distraught man, Mr. Shore."

"Oh, I don't think so, Lisa," he said. "That letter I got from him about that cop who shot the boy. A good-humored, amusing letter. Called him 'our cop.' That letter didn't come from a distraught man."

"Al's clever. Far too clever to sound distraught writing to you."

"Well, when I answer his letter—"

"Yes, but where will you send the letter?"

146

"Ah, yes, I see," and he looked at his glass which was empty. Turning to the table for another drink, he stood with his back to her, pouring. She couldn't take her eyes off him. He had good strong shoulders. The curling iron-gray hair was a little long on his neck. His unlined face, with not a wrinkle in it, had a high color and in him was a kind of relaxed power. Looking at the drink he had poured, he sipped it and leaned back in the big wing chair. Behind him on the wall was a small Modigliani, a beautiful, long-necked girl. Shore's head was just beneath the serene girl's head.

"A man has to be alone to concentrate, Lisa," he said. "At this stage maybe Al feels he has to be by himself, all by himself in his concentration. I've been this way myself. It's quite normal. Or maybe Al feels he's alone with you too much."

She got up and went over to a stool beside his chair and sat, hunching her knees up, her arms around them, her head close to his leg, and she began to make a pattern with her finger on the stool. "Al's never really alone with me now," she said softly.

"Aren't you living together?"

"It sounds strange, doesn't it?"

"It does."

"It is," she said and thought she was going to cry. "This last little while has been an agony. He's out walking or in his room. I have to listen and feel his terrible absorption. Even when he comes to bed and I try to put my arms around him, it's no good. I feel something else in the back of his mind." She drew back, trying to joke brightly. "You, Mr. Shore. Ah, Mr. Shore, you shouldn't be there in bed with us, should you?"

"It must be dreadful for you, Lisa." She had leaned forward closer to him. Her head was close to his knee. He went to touch her head, then he flushed and burst out irritably, "These academics. Their crazy training. It's a wonder any of them are left with any minds of their own. I avoid them. But Al—he's different. He's very bright. Why in hell can't he finish the thing?"

"I don't know. Maybe it's you."

147

"Me?"

"He knows you're around to correct him. I'm not sure of anything now. Neither is Al."

"He's sure of you, isn't he?"

"I think I'm the only thing he's sure of."

"Yet he runs from you."

"Am I that unattractive, Mr. Shore? Am I?" Her voice broke, and she got up before he could answer, picked up her drink, finished it, and sat down on the couch, hanging her head.

"Lisa," he said. When she didn't answer, he got up and went over to her. "Lisa," he said, sounding a little sad as he looked at her somberly. "Al will forgive you, Lisa," but she couldn't fathom the look in his eyes, then he turned as if her eyes were carrying him off to other places. "This is my wife's home, Lisa," he said.

"I know."

"Soon I'll be off by myself, to Paris or Rome."

"Will you?"

"I suppose a part of me is forever lonely. But my wife understands me."

"I know."

"This is our protected place. My wife has humor. From her I learned gentleness of touch and the sweet smell of a woman's flesh. I learned so many things about people being together." Then, as if wondering why he was offering these words to the wild, distraught girl looking up at him, waiting and shaking him, he said with sudden emotion: "You don't seem to belong around here, Lisa. Oh, maybe you do now; I don't know. But whatever you are, wherever it is, you'll be forgiven. A girl like you always is. All through history they've been forgiven, because . . . well, it's a kind of burning generosity of love in you, Lisa. Maybe too much for a man to handle."

"If that's the way I am, it's the way I am," she murmured, sighing. "Well, no one burns for me." Her knees were close together, her arms wrapped around them, her head hung to one side, the left cheek down, her black hair falling to her knees as

148

she stared down at her shoes. They were tan alligator shoes with bluntly rounded toes, the shoes she had bought last week. Al said she paid too much money for them.

"This is a very nice rug," she said, frowning. "Is it Spanish?"

"A Spanish design. It's really an Indian rug."

"Is it?" Then looking up, distressed, she said: "I go on like this. After all, you didn't ask to come into our lives or even to be a spectator."

"A spectator," he said, sitting down beside her. "A spectator of what?"

"Of Al and me."

"Now Lisa. Before I ever saw Al he was in trouble with his work. You told me so."

"I know I did."

"I liked Al. Why, I tried to make myself available. In spite of any natural instinct."

"Just what did you do? The more available you were, the less he seemed to know."

"About what, Lisa?"

"Your view, your work."

"I don't explain myself."

"No! So it's been interesting, hasn't it?"

"Al's interesting, yes."

"Al?" she asked softly, reproving him, as if from the beginning they had known they had some more secret understanding. "It must have been interesting watching how your work demoralized him. God, he's a strange man now."

"Are you sure, Lisa? I'm not. I've thought about him and wondered. You see, I have a terrible curiosity about people."

"Yes, I remember. You said you'd be very curious."

"And I was."

"That's it," she said, sighing. "Just your curiosity."

"It's my life, Lisa."

"You're curious about me now, too," she said, smiling faintly. "Aren't you?"

"Of course I am."

149

"How far does it go with me?"

"Now, Lisa," he said uneasily.

"Well, I know. Yes, I think I knew from the beginning."

"You're a beautiful girl," he said gently as he regarded her, then slowly he came bending down over her, just looking at her face. He took her face in both his hands, holding it almost reverently in the stillness. In his eyes there was such an intensity of appreciation, such yearning and lasting wonder, that she was afraid to breathe, break the moment, lose that look, lose the feel of her face in his hands. Then she shivered. She had to reach out, her arms going around him compulsively. He came down on her, then she felt his heart beating. Everything was breaking up for her. As she held him, she thought she would cry.

His hands, on her breasts at first, were now on her chest as he firmly pushed himself up and away from her. When he stood up, smoothing his coat, their eyes met. He drew back farther, as no man touching her had ever drawn back. For a moment he was too troubled, then he shook his head, half angrily.

Her face began to burn, then she wanted to strike out at him blindly.

"No, never mind, Lisa," he said. The gentle, protective hug he gave her as he lifted her up was unbearably humiliating, and she felt sick. "I'm not myself," she whispered.

"Yes, you are, Lisa," he said. "It's all you. . . . What happens with me is nothing to you. It shouldn't trouble you. Come on, forget it."

"Al was wrong about one thing," she said jerkily. "He said you have no egotism. You're all ego, aren't you?"

"That may well be. It may very well be," he said, leaving her standing there, confused, alone, while he walked up and down with a little smile. Finally he turned. "I'll tell you what I'll do, Lisa," he said. "I'll call this Fulton and tell him that I'm doing a story about this city for the *World*."

"Thank you," she whispered, trying to smile.

"Good night, Lisa."

"Good night," she said. She fled along the street to her car.

150

A neighbor, watering his lawn, looked quickly at her and the Shore house. Her humiliation deep and terrible, Lisa walked on blindly past the car, a hundred yards farther, then she turned, looking around, thinking it had been stolen. Then she saw it by the curb farther back and ran to it and got in. "Oh, Al, I wish I didn't love you so much," she whispered, closing her eyes. Even in the car she couldn't feel hidden. As she drove away Shore was there in her thoughts, drawing back with that unbearable smile of contempt—for himself, not her.

20

Coming along the dark alley from the garage to the front of the house, her heels clicking loudly, Lisa opened the front door. Then she heard the sound upstairs, the squeaking sound of a door closing. She was scared. In the neighborhood recently there had been many burglaries. Climbing the stairs slowly, she called out: "Is that you, Al?" just to make it appear to an intruder that she was expecting someone.

"Yeah, it's me," Al called from the kitchen.

She couldn't believe it was really Al and stood on the stairs, trembling nervously, ready to run. Then he came out to the hall. "Hello, Lisa," he said.

"Al! It's really you!"

"Sure it's me. Well, it's your place. Come on up."

"I didn't know who it might be," she said, shocked to think that Mr. Shore could get word to him so soon, then her common sense told her that Mr. Shore couldn't have done it. He hadn't had time. Al must have returned to her of his own accord. The surge of relief and joy in her made her feel weak; she could hardly climb the stairs. "How are you, Al?" she said, breathlessly, following him into the living room.

"I'm fine." Gaunt and pale though he was, he was clean,

153

and he had the same funny little crooked smile. His long hair was carefully combed, his beard trimmed neatly, and he had on a clean shirt. "And how are you, Lisa?" he asked, sitting down.

"Al, I'm sorry I wasn't here."

"Why should you be here?"

"Why, to hear you coming up the stairs."

"I phoned earlier. You weren't here."

"No, no—Al." She smiled. "I was talking to Mr. Shore."

"He phoned here?"

"I phoned him, Al. I saw him."

"At his place. Oh, my God, Lisa."

"Oh, Al darling, darling," and she tried to laugh.

"God, how embarrassing. How could you, Lisa?"

"Al, you've got it it all wrong," she said brightly. "Now wait. Listen. I phoned him. I told him we had decided you should go off somewhere by yourself to work. Even I wasn't to know where. See?" She didn't feel she was lying. She thought she was sparing him something he wouldn't understand. "That was the idea. Oh, Al, that's what I said. But when I started to worry, and I wondered if Mr. Shore had heard from you, he understood. Al—he said drop in if I wanted to talk, and I did feel better. Al . . . Al . . . I was so terribly worried. It was like going to meet you. He had on a jacket like one I wanted to get you—"

"Lisa—" but he didn't finish. His eyes showed his pained, desperate protest against his affectionate understanding of her. Sighing, he said mildly, "Well, and how is Mr. Shore?"

"Fine, Al. You know, he's a very friendly man. And he was glad to get your letter. It amused him. He likes you, Al." She was trying to get Shore out of the way, get him out of her mind so Al could throw his arms around her. "Let me get you a cup of coffee," she said.

"Okay," he said and followed her into the kitchen. While she was making the coffee he got the evening newspaper. "What's going on in the world?" he said, turning the pages. He sounded just like himself, always late in looking at the newspaper. So often he had sat just where he was now, reading. She

154

understood that it was important that she should not ask where he had been. He talked idly about the war news. "Let me bum one of your cigarettes," he said. He never had his own cigarettes. He smoked, sipped his coffee, and read. "So Mr. Shore liked my letter about the cop," he said suddenly.

"He thought it was amusing. He wanted to answer it."

"Why didn't he?"

"I guess he will."

"What's holding him back?"

"You know, Al," she said, her elbows on the table, her chin in her cupped hands. "Talking about Shore, I had a hunch about that man. I had it watching and listening to him. The Shore philosophy! The Shore view of life! What's a philosophy, Al? Who the hell cares about a philosophy these days? I mean, that's what I was thinking in my own kooky way, listening to him." Smiling, waiting, smiling again, she longed to be able to quicken him. "Any intellectual mechanic can hammer out some kind of a fixed philosophy. You know that. Well, that's when I had my hunch. And I said to myself, 'this man hasn't got any view of life at all. Just some kind of a view of himself, not life, just himself.' Is that crazy, Al?"

"No, it's not crazy," he said. But in spite of himself he was silent and wondering.

"What does it mean, Al? Or does it mean anything?"

"I'm not sure what it would mean."

"Is it even worth thinking about?"

"I'll think about it," he said, and he sat reflecting on her observation, a simple observation not pushed at him at all. It was a hushed and beautiful moment for her, watching him meditate. Suddenly he said, "Well, I must be on my way, Lisa."

"On your way? Where?"

"I just dropped in, Lisa."

"You're not staying?"

"I wanted to pick up my notes and all," he said. As they both got up, she was bewildered, following him as he went along the hall. If he had only turned he would have seen the panic in her, but he went into his room. She watched him open

155

drawers, take out those folders containing his notes, and all her typing too, clearing out the drawers, cleaning off the desk all his work on Eugene Shore. While he took his briefcase from the cupboard and opened it, she stood with her arms folded, and her head back, trembling, yet controlling her outrage. Then she thought, he must not put those folders in the briefcase; he must not close the bag. "Where do you think you're taking that stuff, Al?" she asked.

"Where I can work," he said.

"All that work was done here, Al."

"So what? It's my work. I'm not leaving it here."

"Oh, yes you are, Al."

"Lisa, I told you. . . ."

"To hell with it. Don't let that man do this to us, Al," she said desperately. "That domineering man isn't going to do it, Al." Pausing, looking at her in astonishment, he said: "Isn't going to do what?" Grimly he reached for the file of folders, but she snatched them away, backing around the desk.

Astonished, he laughed, "Oh, come on, Lisa; cut it out."

But she kept backing away from him, backing around the desk. They circled the desk twice. She kept the folders clutched to her breast. When he grabbed she banged his hand away. "Are you out of your mind?" he said. "I've had enough," and he closed the door. Very calmly he put the chair at one end of the desk, trapping her just as if he were cornering an excited dog. Then he came around the desk slowly. She went to jump on the couch and circled the chair, but he got her in the corner, the couch behind her, the window to her left. Just as she was ready to fall on the couch, clutching the folders, and sob brokenly, he jumped at her. The fury in his face revived her spirit. He got her by the shoulders; his fingers digging into her flesh made her cry out in pain. She tried to hit him with the folders, shrieking, "You damn fool. Never." She hurled the heavy folders at the window, shattering the pane. The folders with all their loose papers went out the window. They heard the flopping sound in the alley below.

"Why, you bitch," he yelled and came at her, knocking her

156

back on the couch, knocking the chair over that was between the couch and the desk and got her by the throat. As she clawed at his hair, her sudden fear, exciting her wildly, made her strain with her whole being, gasping and choking yet wanting to sob from feeling him on her, over all of her, while the breath died in her. Then suddenly his grip on her throat relaxed, and he was still. Trembling, ready to burst into tears, yet holding and clinging to him, she looked up.

"My God," he whispered stricken, and he stood up slowly. "And they used to call me the champ." He had an expression on his face that she had never seen before—hatred of the loss of all sense of himself. Then, in a proud gathering together that bewildered her, he drew away and made her think of Shore, too, drawing back, made Shore seem to be all around her, smothering her, and she shrieked, "Get the hell out of here. Get out. I'll grab something. I'll kill you."

"Lisa," he said. "I'm sorry. I expected nothing like this." Calm under her threat, and under the pressure of the violence within him, he turned to go, then, held by her fierce, wild eyes, he stood staring, as if at last he had got a glimpse of her that shook his imagination. He half reached out to her, looking much bigger himself, and more dominant, then, pulling away, he went without saying another word.

21

Earlier there had been strong morning sunlight, but it had clouded up and by ten, when Al was on the steps of the old City Hall, it started to rain. As he moved back into the shelter of the main arch, he saw Mr. Shore come hurrying from the department store to the left, looking like a bank president caught in the rain in his double-breasted brown suit and Cardin hat. He broke into a little trot. He came up the steps, puffing hard, his pink face glowing.

"How are you, Al? I wondered if you'd be here." And he drew back looking at him closely. "Why, you look good, Al," he said. But Al had caught the questioning appraisal. What did Lisa say about me? he wondered, going along the corridor to the courtroom where the inquest was being held. "I'm still puffing. I can't be in very good shape," Shore said. "I walked all the way down to get some exercise. I need it. I was sure it wasn't going to rain." When they had turned into another corridor where a little crowd was filing into the courtroom, he said, "I thought Lisa might be here with you."

"She couldn't make it," Al said. They were now in the old oak paneled courtroom. They found seats on the rear bench beside two sedate, elderly Puerto Ricans. It was a well-attended inquest. In the second row was Juan's mother, a short, heavy, tired, scared woman. Beside her was Tony Gonzalez in a dark suit he obviously didn't like wearing. Behind them were young members of the small Panamanian community, ill at ease and shabby, as well as three better-dressed, sedate, middle-aged men who looked very stern. Four uniformed policemen sat together. There were 20 other men and women who seemed to be out of nowhere, all waiting for the coroner to arrive.

"I understand Lisa dropped in on you," Al said.

"Yes, she did. I was glad to see her."

"How did she seem to you?"

"Very much like herself. Are you worried about Lisa?"

"She thinks I'm blowing my career."

"I think she'll come around, Al."

"I think she's a little distraught," Al said guardedly, trying to smile. "If you were writing about Lisa, I don't know what you'd make of her right now . . . or where you'd place her. But maybe you do know."

The coroner's constable was calling the court to order, then the coroner, Dr. Baldwin, came in. He was a tall, well-built man of 50, with thick, black hair combed back tightly, and wearing a double-breasted dark suit with a pin stripe. He looked well-fed, like a man who was on good terms with himself. He was at home here, too. He had been a star college football player, much more successful as a football player than as a doctor, but everyone knew him and liked him and he had got the coroner's job.

He was smiling encouragingly at his jurymen, who were like fruit from the same vine, all about the same age—in their fifties—all scrupulously clean, all gravely earnest about their job, all determined to have a clean conscience to the best of their abilities; and they all looked like property-owners.

Two lawyers, not on convivial terms, sat at a table in front of the coroner's bench. The older one was Henry Ralston, assigned to assist the coroner. His colleague, J. Robertson Dunton, 25 years old, sincere, with a passion for civil liberties, had offered his services to the Gonzalez family.

160

"But where's our cop?" Shore whispered.

Dr. Baldwin, who had been studying some notes, looked up and in a grave, troubled tone outlined the purpose of the inquest. The jury, hearing all the facts, circumstances, and any witnesses who could be helpful in getting at the truth, was to determine how and by what means an unfortunate young man came to his death.

"There's your friend now," Al whispered.

Jason Dunsford had slipped into the room with Ira Mustard. In his civilian clothes, a gray suit and a dark blue tie, he had a massive self-assurance. He had gained in presence; he now had the air of an important man. He had had a haircut. Ira Mustard had had one too: the good, bright, clean haircuts of men with nothing to hide.

As Jason folded his arms, the brother of Juan Gonzalez stood up, glaring, and grabbed his mother's arm beside him. She tugged at his sleeve angrily. The coroner said, "Thank you, madam" and looked at the long windows. The rain was streaming down the panes. It fell so heavily that the streets must have been flooding.

Mr. Ralston, rising, said helpfully: "Juan Gonzalez. The deceased is Juan Gonzalez," as if the coroner might never have heard of the young man. Ralston's tone suggested that there might have been some doubt in his own mind about the young man's existence. Now something had to be found out about him. The coroner called on Juan's mother.

The short, scared woman of 60, her face puffed from crying, spoke haltingly. Under Mr. Ralston's gentle prompting she told something about herself. She had been born in Panama and had been here in town two years. She earned her living as a cleaning woman. Yes, at times she had been on welfare. She had two sons—Juan, 24, and Tony, 18. Juan had been an assistant to a shipper in a candy factory. Yes, once he had been on welfare. But he hadn't liked it. He earned $72 a week. All this last year he had worked and had never had trouble with the police.

So it was established that there had been such a boy as Juan

Gonzalez. Mr. Ralston suggested to the coroner that he would like to have the police record. He called on Inspector Sutherland who read the report that Officer Dunsford had turned in. The inspector told of Jason's condition at the station the night of the shooting and about Jason's astonishment, his vast surprise, his shock, his dreamlike disbelief that he hadn't been maimed or shot at himself. It was a good, quiet picture of a distraught officer. The inspector said they had made powder tests on the slain man which showed how close he had been to the officer.

"Is Officer Mustard here?" Mr. Ralston asked.

"Here, sir," Ira said.

"Look at that fellow," Shore whispered. "Isn't he wonderful? That head. That chin. Already I believe everything he's going to say."

Ira Mustard had a bluff sincerity. Sometimes he would hesitate a little, screwing up his eyes as he corrected himself, trying to get every detail, everything just as it had happened that night. "It was raining," he said. "Almost as heavily as it is now," and he looked at the windows. But even here he corrected himself. "No, sir, not that heavily or we wouldn't have been able to see at all. Who could chase a car the way it's coming down now?" And then, taking his time, he told about the chase and about the shooting in the dark near the old garage.

The coroner, who had glanced at his watch, observed that it was past noon. The inquest would be adjourned till two o'clock, and he looked in surprise at the window. The rain had suddenly stopped. The sun had come out.

As they were filing into the corridor, one of the newspapermen, Bob Gowdy, recognized Shore, noticeable in that little crowd as the one who was expensively dressed, the only one who suggested that he didn't have to care where he was. "Aren't you Eugene Shore?" Gowdy asked. Mr. Shore smiled faintly. Gowdy said, "What's a man like you doing here? What's the angle? What's your interest, Mr. Shore?"

"I'm a citizen and a taxpayer," Mr. Shore said blandly. "I

should be here, shouldn't I?" He patted Gowdy on the shoulder. "Al," he said, turning to him, "why don't we go over to the Colonial and have a drink and some lunch? What about it?"

"I certainly could use a drink," Al said.

Outside, puddles glittered brilliantly. The sun came from a bright patch of blue high over Simpson's tower. On the way to the Colonial, they cut through Eaton's Department Store. In the dimly lighted lounge they had two martinis each. Shore had a good lunch of breaded veal cutlets, and urged Al to try them after he had finished the salad he ordered. When they were having their coffee, Shore asked, "How's the work going, Al?"

"Could I ask you one simple little question? It may give me the key to your work."

"Go ahead. Anything."

"This is a little corny, I know. It's a point I'm at in my work. How do you see yourself?"

"How do I see myself? Why, I don't see myself at all."

"You must have some view of yourself."

"Why must I?"

"Every man sees himself in a certain light," Al persisted. "Every man has some view of himself."

"Not me, Al."

"Now you're kidding me."

"No, Al. Listen. I don't *want* to have a view of myself." Smiling cynically, Al said nothing. "I'm on the level, Al."

"It doesn't sound right."

"I know," Shore said, but he was silent, reflecting. "Maybe I should have been a painter," he said after a pause. "I used to say to myself, 'Painting is the thing.' Yet I didn't paint. I wrote. Something was always wrong with what I wrote. I threw it all away. I was about 25 and living alone. Well, one night after midnight, I was at my window. It overlooked a little park flooded with moonlight, and I stood idly looking out. In my line of vision there was a tree and a drinking fountain. Suddenly that tree was there with an astonishing reality—coming right up close to me. I saw it as I had never seen it before, and I was

163

moved, deeply moved and then fascinated. Why this moving clarity? Then I realized that I hadn't been saying to myself, 'There's a tree. How should I see it? How would Flaubert see it?' No, standing at the window without a thought in my head, I had forgotten I existed, so I was there. All of me exposed to that object, all of me there without any awareness of myself, all of me hanging together, receptive just to the thing as it was—and the wonder of it—being just as it was. The wonder of separate things. And this is funny, Al. Not thinking about myself, I seemed to come all together." Then he caught the expression on Al's face and shrugged. "Well, Al, it's the truth."

"It's not what I asked you, Mr. Shore."

"It's the root of the matter."

"I can't imagine a man more aware of himself."

"Well, have it your way, Al."

"Your way—the tree and all that stuff—it's too nebulous."

"Not to me."

"Stuff comes at you. You take it in, and you make it sound mysterious," Al said. "*Is* it so mysterious?"

"What's the matter with a little mystery?"

"It's not my way. It tells me nothing."

"Alright," Shore said. "Call it just a heightened sense of life. How's that?"

"Not so good, either," Al said, but even as he smiled, he thought: *Wait a minute. He may really be telling me something about his work and his life.* Then Al's imagination took a leap. Those moments of wonder, the sudden impact of the reality of things, that same kind of wonder was in all Shore's work. But about people, not trees! Each person made as clearly special as his tree seen that night. A man waiting at a window. But really waiting for his favorite people, those fiercely stubborn characters, those self-directed exiles from society, to loom up suddenly and come into his imagination. Their haven! Their temple, where he offered them warmth and respect for being just what they were. Why? Was it because such people had something unexpected in them, the wild unpredictability he loved? For

164

being just as they were? Like his tree? No. In his keeping, in his haven, in some mysterious way, they unexpectedly became bigger, more human, higher up than they were, knowing they could make it in his world.

"No," Al burst out vehemently.

"No, what?" Shore asked.

"Taking in trees, taking in people, taking them in and giving them some kind of benediction. No," Al protested, leaning closer. "Just what are you? Your own church?"

"Alright," Shore said, shrugging. "I'm my own church."

"But look what you do. . . ."

"What do I do?"

"I mean with your view, what you'd have to do."

"What would I have to do?"

"This cop—I think he's capable of anything now."

"So do I."

"Look," Al insisted, "there's something wrong here. You'd take that man into your church and respect him for being just what he is because he can go wild and be capable of anything, the way you like them—exciting—and maybe you'd warm him up and make him into one of your big human beings with no one knowing what big grand thing he'd do next. Well, there's something wrong here, something all wrong. You'd be putting plain old criminal thievery in the odor of sanctity. Well, I'm sorry, Mr. Shore. That's not real life. It's not a view of life. It's just your own temperament. And it's just sentimental to make that guy anything but the thug and killer he is."

"Well, I'm sure he's a liar," Shore said mildly. "As yet, I don't know where I'd put him. I don't know what's gone on in his life. And neither do you, Al. Neither do you. Real lives, you say?"

When Shore leaned back, Al tried to hold his eyes, hold him where he had finally got him. He waited, knowing Shore was pondering something.

"I think you've got me a little wrong," he said at last. "Just a little wrong, Al." Then he looked at his watch. "We'd better

165

be getting back to that inquest. It may have started. What do you say?" Standing up, he gave Al an affectionate pat on the shoulder.

They came out of the darkened bar into the sunlight, walking slowly. The City Hall steps were now dry. On a scaffolding high on the tower some workmen were cleaning the grimy stone. The clock in the tower had stopped—either that or it had lost time. It said nine o'clock.

22

The coroner looked as if he had had a good lunch and a few drinks with some friends. His voice was a little stronger, and he had a new, even more comforting, authority. And Mr. Ralston, too, when he said he thought they should now hear from Officer Dunsford, made everyone in the room believe it had just occurred to him that Jason Dunsford, a cop, might just possibly be helpful.

Jason had the worried look of a big man who can afford to be accurate about every little detail that might be helpful. The whole city ought to know why he had shot Juan Gonzalez. The magisterial tone he had been cultivating for years helped him now. He repeated Mustard's story about the men in the car refusing to stop; they had cursed and jeered. "We were sure we had the men we were after. It was a blue car," he said. "They were doing some pretty fancy driving to get away, and they nearly made it, too. A minute later and we would never have seen that taillight turning into the garage. In the rain and the dark we saw the two men getting out of a car at the side of the garage."

"Now how far away were you from their car?" Mr. Ralston asked.

"I would say 25 feet, sir."

"Did you have your gun in your hand?"

"I did, sir. I called out, 'Come forward with your hands up.' Officer Mustard had his flashlight on them."

"One moment, officer," the coroner said. "Is it possible that these two young men, blinded by the glare of the flashlight, could not see the gun in your hand?"

"Quite possible, sir."

"Under a flashlight, the man that is seen can hardly see you. He might have believed you were unarmed?"

"Something like that, yes, sir."

"Thank you, officer. Go on."

"So they came forward," Jason said. "The bigger one started yelling, something about it being his car. He kept coming closer. Real close, his hand went to his breast pocket. Real close, he whipped his hand out. Something was in his hand and he was almost on me. So I fired. He fell." Jason had lowered his head; now he jerked it back. "He was there in the mud and the rain, and there was something in his hands alright. But the thing he had pulled out was only a wallet."

"He swung it at you?"

"A swinging motion at me," Jason said, and then, as if he were trying only to get at the truth: "I can see now it might have been a show-off gesture."

"Why should he be showing off?"

"Well, if he didn't like the police, and this time he knew we had nothing on him."

"Clowning?"

"It could be that, sir."

"But he was coming at you, he got that close to you?"

"Yes, sir."

"Have you anything to add?"

"That's all there was to it."

"Thank you, officer."

The only other witness was Tony Gonzalez. Small, dark, and uncomfortable in his suit, he stood with his angry, excited eyes on Jason.

168

"Can I say something?" he blurted out. "This is all wrong, Mr. Coroner. Why don't this lawyer ask that cop why he killed Juan?"

"Tony," his mother cried and jumped up. "No, Tony, no. Quiet, you come here. We go home," as if she wanted to get him out of that room before he too could be snatched away. The coroner asked an officer to speak to her. Officer McCurdy, gray, over 60, and due for his pension, soothed her gently. The coroner cautioned Tony in a warm, comforting manner. He mustn't blurt out things. Did he understand? Just tell what happened.

"I sure will," the boy said belligerently. He told about driving with his brother from the party. It had been a great party, lots of wine, lots of jokes. No fights. "We were driving along in the rain," he said. "This other crazy car kept swinging over to us. How could we know they was cops in that car? The big beefy face shouting at us. 'Some crazy drunks, eh, kid?' Juan said. So we shouted, too. It happens again. They shout. We shout. How can we hear what they say? How can we see? Drunks. It's not a police car. It's not marked. Juan was great with a car. 'Watch me shake those jerks,' he said, and he left them behind, and we were laughing, and we get to the lot by the old garage. We get out of the car laughing and happy. Making jokes and these two big guys come at us. That guy there," he said, pointing at Jason, "had a gun. Juan is not scared. Why be scared? We do nothing wrong. We laugh. Maybe they think the car stolen. Okay. Juan can laugh. He has his license. 'Here, I show you,' he yells. He is taking it out of his pocket. He is ten feet away. Not up close. Not up close at all. Ten feet, I say. Bang. Juan's dying there." Trembling, the boy pointed at Jason. "That man murdered my brother. Murderer!" he shouted, "murderer!"

"Here, that will do," the coroner shouted.

But now there was an air of embarrassment in the room. The five jurymen shifted uncomfortably. Al said to Shore: "I feel it, Mr. Shore. Something's in this atmosphere here. Am I right?" Shore, not answering, kept his eyes on Jason Dunsford who sat with his arms folded, his head jerking back, then back

169

again. "Only camels work their heads back and then back like that," Shore whispered. "Men usually lower their heads, then raise them."

"Just a minute," Ralston said to Tony. "You're not excused yet. Thank you. You don't like policemen, do you?"

"Me? I don't know any policemen."

"Come now. You hate the police, don't you?"

"They don't know me; I don't know them."

"And your brother hated the police, didn't he?"

"Cops? He knew no cops."

"Supposing I tell you that I can find witnesses, your friends, who would say you jeered and reviled policemen every chance you got? What is it you call them—'fuzz from the cop shop'?"

"Good heavens," Dunton shouted, jumping up. "What is this? What kind of cheap stunt is this? There's not a mark against this boy or his dead brother. What are you trying to do? Disgrace them? Is this boy supposed to be a hostile witness? This is not a trial."

"Yes, where are you going, Mr. Ralston?" the coroner asked.

"I think we should know the psychology, the frame of mind, of the deceased, the contempt he showed by shouting from his car. His contempt when he approached the policemen," Mr. Ralston said mildly. "That's all."

"Oh no, it isn't," Tony said. "There's something else."

"Something you saw?" the coroner asked. "Now be careful. It must be something you saw."

"Wasn't I there?" Tony asked bitterly. "It's this. Juan could not have got that close to him on account of the barrels. Juan couldn't get that close."

The coroner, looking thoughtfully at Mr. Ralston, left it up to him. The jury also watched Mr. Ralston. Smiling reassuringly at the jury, he said, "Obviously we should hear from Officer Mustard again. Officer Mustard, come forward. Officer, you didn't mention the barrels," Ralston said bluntly. "Why not? Were these barrels there?"

"Come to think of it, some old barrels were lying around. I didn't think they had anything to do with it."

"Were these barrels a kind of barrier between the deceased and Officer Dunsford?"

"Barrier? It's news to me."

"Would the deceased have had to get over the barrels to get at the officer?"

Ira looked surprised. "Why, those barrels were over to one side," he said. "Yeah, that's right," finally placing the barrels in his mind to his own satisfaction. "Over to one side, yes. In the way—oh no, sir."

"Thank you, officer," the coroner said. "Well, unless someone else wants to come forward—"

"Sir," J. Robertson Dunton said sharply to the coroner. "I've been retained by Juan's family. But even if I have no place at such an inquest, nevertheless, as a friend of the court or a friend of the truth—"

"That'll do, sir," the coroner said. "You have no right to be here at all."

"Indeed, I do have a right."

"You have no inherent right."

"There may be a civil suit."

"I've been allowing you a certain leeway, sir," the coroner said, growing more amiable. "Now please sit down. Thank you." When the coroner asked again if anyone had anything to add that might be helpful and there was no response, Mr. Ralston approached him, and they consulted. A little flush appeared on the coroner's face as he went over his notes. Clearing his throat, he spoke boldly and determinedly, sounding like a judge or a man who had always wanted to be a judge—not a doctor, another man in the wrong place. Going over the evidence, he pointed out that there was no doubt about the gun being in Officer Dunsford's hand and that he had fired the gun. But if it wasn't an inadvertent firing, a firing by the officer in the course of his duty in the belief that his own life was threatened, a man reacting involuntarily to the threat, then it was a deliberate murder. Could it be that the whole thing was an inadvertent

171

occurrence? If there had been no threatening gesture and the young man had been ten feet away, the officer would be open to a charge of murder. But why would an officer fire his gun in those circumstances? So in their conclusion they had to face this fact. If it was a wilful killing, a murder had been committed. It was that—or an inadvertent, accidental death. What other choice was there? The coroner now fumbled his words, but kept repeating this central choice. They should bear in mind that as a result of their deliberations an officer might face a murder charge. Pausing, contemplating his clenched hands, he shook his head gravely, then abandoning his instructive legal tone, he became a comforting doctor again. He hoped he had been helpful. The jury filed out.

"Good God, I certainly need a drink now, Al," Mr. Shore said. "How about you?"

"Can we wash *that* stuff down with a drink?"

"It's what the coroner will try and do as soon as he gets to his office, isn't it? Come on."

On the way over to the bar, Shore was silent and troubled. In the bar he gulped down a brandy. His bland amiability was gone. His face suddenly had its own hard strength. "Law and order, eh?" he said softly. "Why is it, Al, that law and order are so often destructive of all natural justice? That cop with his gun is law and order. Coroner's juries! Dummies! Nothing must be allowed to happen to weaken our respect for the cop's gun."

"I know how I'd reckon it. I'd get a bigger gun."

"Well, I'm not a pacifist myself, either, Al."

"You sure aren't," Al said. He wondered whether Shore was outraged by the lack of respect shown the boys or whether he had it in for that cop who had insulted him.

When they got back to the City Hall corridor newspapermen, family friends, and policemen still waited. The jury was obviously having some difficulty reaching a conclusion. The courtroom was empty. The hard oak bench was uncomfortable.

"A lot of my life was within two blocks of this neighborhood," Shore said, calm and patient now. But he was talking about his own life. Al was suddenly alert and expectant. Shore began to tell amusing stories about being articled to a lawyer in an office just a block away. The lawyers in that office had been young and poor, with lots of time on their hands, so it had been a scandalous place in a hilarious time. He could make anything into an amusing story; he had the captivating touch. But after a pause, he said: "at lunch I found myself thinking of you and Lisa."

"Lisa?" Al said uneasily. "I suppose you gathered it's not so good with us right now."

"I did get that impression, yes."

"These days," Al said, trying to smile. "I always seem to be saying, 'Where's Lisa?'"

"And all the time she's right beside you?"

"I suppose so."

"Hmmm," Shore said, and he smiled and nodded. "It must be interesting. 'Where is Lisa?' Yes, I like that. I'm sure there's strange wild stuff in that girl you'd never expect from her manner. Well, I've liked wondering and writing about people like her. I suppose you've noticed. I'm sure you have—" But he saw the coroner coming from his office. "Well, here they are, Al," he said. The lawyers came in, and almost at once the jury filed in. The coroner asked if they had agreed on a verdict.

They had, the foreman said. Their verdict was that Juan Gonzalez had come to his death when shot by Officer Dunsford and that the death had been inadvertent.

"Hey, what is this?" Tony Gonzalez gasped, and he jumped up and shouted, "No," and he said to the family lawyer, "Hey, you say something. Come on." The young lawyer said sternly, "Shh Shh. There can still be proceedings." The boy's mother, grabbing him, hurried him out.

A little crowd lingered in the corridor, and among them were some newspapermen. An elderly police reporter who was heard every day on the radio joined Shore and Al. "I spoke to the jury foreman," he said. "A worried man. But what the hell? The coroner gave them no other choice."

"Why didn't they say to hell with the coroner?" Al said.

"Are you kidding? He's an accountant. Accountants don't

173

say publicly to hell with coroners. That would be a bad item in the books."

"Mr. Shore, I don't see how you can write this story," Al said. "Nobody will want to print that."

"I'm sure they'll print it and just as I write it," Shore said. "As long as it isn't libelous, and I'm very good at avoiding libel." Then his face lit up. He sounded like a young man. "I've a picture in my head right now. Shadows. The inquest, a place in the shadows. Masked men waiting in the shadows. The cop and his pals, just eyes above the masks. The coroner in a mask and the jurymen and that bland lawyer, too. The only face that isn't masked is the mother's—all ancient human suffering mirrored in her face as the mask men peer at her."

"Good God, you make them sound like hold-up men."

"Well, they are, Al. Hold-up men and a rescue party. They rescued their cop, didn't they?" and he laughed. Al laughed with him.

A newspaper photographer came brushing past and said, "Excuse me." His camera was on the entrance. The coroner came out. Beside him, listening amiably while the coroner talked, was Jason Dunsford. Two big men. The coroner at ease in the security marked out for him here in town, and Jason, a little stiffer in body, a little heavier, his neat clothes not up to the doctor's expensive suit. Yet they shared one thing for the camera: a big, complacent grin. As Jason's head went back, his grin widened from exultant satisfaction into indulgent contempt for the rigamarole of vindication of his act.

"They're grinning! Look at them. That should scare the wits out of people," Al said. "Two thugs."

"They are," Shore said.

They went outside and stood at the top of the wide steps where other groups waited, saying little, just waiting in the sunlight as if things might soon look better. Mrs. Gonzalez and her son Tony were in earnest conversation with Dunton. Then Jason Dunsford, breaking away from the coroner, came within a few feet of Al on his way to join two plainclothes officers off to the left. For a moment Al was face to face with him, and he

174

nodded. Jason passed by, then apparently aware that he had seen someone he ought to have recognized, he turned, watching.

"Let's see what's going on here," Shore said, and they joined the group gathering around the lawyer. Al knew that Jason Dunsford, standing there, making his friends come over to him,, was watching, and he didn't like it. He was sure that Jason hadn't felt threatened. He was sure Jason had felt compelled to shoot the boy. The lawyer was trying to get away from three elderly, sedately dressed Panamanians who took turns talking rapidly to each other in Spanish. Shore listened attentively. Had he picked up some Spanish in his travels, Al wondered. Maybe in Mexico. Tony Gonzalez grabbed the lawyer's arm. The lawyer frowned, looking at Tony's hand. But the violence in the boy's eyes made him careful. "Yes, I said so. Yes, I know I said so," the lawyer repeated. He turned away, and looked across the street. Whichever way he looked, there were banks and trust companies. His office was down the street in one of the few old building left in the neighborhood. "You said it. Civil proceedings," the boy said bitterly. "How do we get these civil proceedings?"

"Mister, mister," Mrs. Gonzalez said apologetically. "Tony is just a boy. He does not understand. Tony, let go the arm."

"Yes, let go," Dunton said gently. "You see, a civil proceeding costs money. A lot of money." The three older Panamanians, having finished their discussion, came a little closer. The one with the deepset eyes and fine nose, bowing a little, said softly: "Excuse me, sir. Money! Sure. There must be money. But our people can raise some money, we can get together. Mrs. Gonzales has her son shot down. The good boy helped support her. She is a poor woman. But we can get together."

"There aren't enough Panamanians in this town to fill a lunch counter," the lawyer said, growing more uncomfortable. "This thing happened here—well—it's the law," and then he took Tony's arm. "You see, son," he said, "the law and justice are sometimes two different things." The helpless rage in

175

Tony's face began to frighten his mother. "Tony, Tony," she said sternly. "We go home quick. We get out of here," offering the lawyer a little nod of acceptance and resignation. "I know these things, mister, but Tony is only an angry boy. I know about the law. Tony does not understand that justice is somewhere else." On her face, lifted in the sunlight, was an expression of resignation born of such an ancient wisdom that Al, startled, looked at Shore and nudged him, but Shore couldn't turn; in his face was a quickening, wondering recognition of something that moved and fascinated him. It was as if he saw that this woman in her hard poverty-stricken life, often fleeing from the law, had kept in her heart an ancient natural concept of justice that allowed her to have some secret respect for herself.

"Good God," Shore said softly, and the change in him, the open involvement now, began to worry Al. His worry showed in his face. "It's okay, Al," Shore said. "I know I've held myself apart around here, but I'll love doing this." Then he turned to the lawyer. "Excuse me," he said "My name is Eugene Shore. I'm doing this story for the *World*. I'll find out what really went on. It'll be quite a story."

"Shore? Did you say Shore?" the lawyer asked, as if he had suddenly placed the name. But Shore, drawing the elderly Panamanians closer, went on, "I want to see Mrs. Gonzalez in her home. Talk to her. Tell her it's important. I want to get a lot of information about that poor dead boy. I want to see that cop, too." In spite of himself, Al turned to see whether Jason Dunsford was still watching them. He was. He had seen him turn and was beckoning. Al pretended he didn't see him.

"When this story is printed," Shore said to the lawyer, "what happened here won't be so easily ignored in this town. And I think you'll find that more people than can fill a lunch counter will want to help out. Of course, it's up to you, Mr. Dunton. I'd like to come and see you. You can be quite a figure in this story," and he shrugged, eyeing the lawyer gravely. People had noticed before that Shore looked like a judge.

"I see, I see," J. Robertson Dunton said, folding his arms

176

over his chest and frowning. He was young and idealistic, but his wife had complained that these cases took up his time, got him no money, and never even got him any attention. Yet now, under Shore's eyes, he seemed to see himself in a brighter light with a big audience. "Alright," he said to the Panamanian who had been the spokesman. "You and your friends be at my office tomorrow at four o'clock." While they were all shaking hands, Al, with Jason still beckoning, went over to him.

"Hello, there," Jason said amiably.

"Hello."

"I didn't expect to see you here."

"Oh, I just dropped in. What do you do when it's raining?"

"Yeah, well, what's he doing here?" and he nodded at Shore. "What's going on?"

"Well, he's a writer, you know."

"I know he's a writer."

"And he's covering this. A big feature story for the *World*'s Sunday supplement."

"I see," Jason said. "So that's what he's up to with those people. Yeah, look at him. He would like those people wouldn't he? Look at them." The lawyer, who had left, was hurrying down the steps. Tony and his mother were talking to Shore. "What's going on?" Jason asked, "come on, tell me."

"I think they're going to raise a fund for a civil suit," Al said. "If they can get enough publicity."

"Shore's to be the publicity, eh? I see." Jason's eyes were still on Shore and the two elderly men. "Why is your friend such a troublemaker, Mr. Delaney? What does he want with those people? Why is he such a traitor to his class?"

"You can ask him," Al said, because Shore, after shaking hands with the two Panamanians, was coming toward them with his little bemused smile and strange sense of ease. Al couldn't see how Shore could have this manner approaching Jason whom he surely must regard as the mortal enemy of everything he stood for. Yet here he was, coming up to them, standing on the step just above Jason and asking easily: "Remember me?"

177

"Yeah," Jason said. "Shore's the name, isn't it?"

"That's right. Look officer, I wonder if you and I could have a talk somewhere. You see, I'm doing a story for the *World*. This unhappy business is part of the story naturally, and you should have a chance to say just what you want to say. In fact, I'd like to see you in your own home. If you have a wife I'd like to talk to her, too. Just human interest stuff."

"You—" Jason didn't say son of a bitch. His eyes had blazed, but he controlled himself. "If I find you near my home. You keep away from my wife and my house." Again, Al, stiffening a little, wondered how Shore could see himself in Jason's home. Yet he would be there if he could, and Jason and his wife, whoever she was, would be treated compassionately and fairly. But in the full story, even if he did not recognize it himself, Jason might appear to be a pitiable thug. And Jason, having got himself in full control, moved up a step beside Shore, looking over him. "No interviews. Regulations. You understand?" He took a few steps toward his waiting colleagues. "Oh, well, you and I have an appointment, anyway," Shore called.

"An appointment?" Jason said, turning.

"A court appointment. I got that summons."

"Oh, hell," Jason said contemptuously. "Why don't you just pay 20 bucks out of court? A busy man like you."

"No, it'll be a kind of interview with you. My second interview. We had one in the snow. Remember? I only want to get to know you a little better. Yes, we'll have our interview," and he shrugged and walked away.

"What the hell is he up to?" Jason said to Al. "Why the hell doesn't he stick to his fairy stories about hookers and priests. Look, tell him to watch out, will you? I've checked him out. He doesn't cut half the ice he thinks he does."

"Yeah, I'll tell him," Al said.

"Just a minute," Jason said and grinned as if he had some vague awareness that he needed Al's goodwill. "Talking about hookers and priests, I've still got something that's your property. That book. I never throw anything away. I'd like your address."

"Bring it to court," Al said. "I'm the witness."

"I can't bring it to court."

"Drop it in the mail, then. I think the address is written on the flyleaf." He walked away and joined Shore. "I just told him I'm the witness," he said. Then full of sudden discontent, he laughed cynically. "The *witness.* That's me. Maybe that's my role in life, Mr. Shore. The scholar! What's a scholar? Another Goddamned witness to someone else's achievements. You know something? When they come to write about you, as they surely will, I'll be in there alright but just as a footnote. The source of an anecdote about a crazy cop. Look, he can't take his eyes off us. Let's go."

23

Those two amiable officers, McBride and Curry, who were offering Jason their sympathetic goodwill there on the City Hall steps, were really offending him. McBride, a redheaded, beer-drinking family man, knew how to do his job and keep out of trouble. Curry was simply a very powerful, good-natured clown. Jason had always looked down on them. They fixed traffic tickets, took little gifts, had friends among crooks. They were little cops who didn't like to see anyone get hurt. The effort at loyalty, coming from such men, now hurt Jason. The acceptance of their goodwill suddenly was beneath him. "Well, so long. Got to get home. Many thanks," he said abruptly, and he left them to get his car from the underground garage.

Jason wanted to be walking alone so he could think, and before he was down the great flight of steps he began to see things clearly.

Shore would make a big splash in the *Evening World*! He, Jason, would be the central figure in that story which would ooze sickly sentimentality for the Gonzalez family. That no-account family would find themselves with a following. A civil suit might bring about a demand for a manslaughter charge. Until now Jason had felt only contempt for Shore, but as he walked along, he thought he saw him as a monstrous source of corruption—the consoler, the redeemer of little thugs like the Gonzalez boy, a man on the side of all that was loose, unprincipled and lawless as he had shown in his crazy book. Then suddenly it came to Jason in an intuitive whisper that Shore would be on the side of Mollie and his wife: the soft sluttish stuff, the drink, the lack of any discipline, of all moral fiber. Shore would make that terrible relationship sound alright, making such things sound good was right up his alley. He was an evil man. All this stuff filling his head told Jason all he wanted to know about Eugene Shore.

Just as he was entering the garage, his mind on the little traffic court case, he stopped, concentrated, and thought he saw something clearly. In the newspaper story, Shore, doing his job, could say whatever he wanted to say about him. That was his aim. Set him up for something. Picture him as a criminal in cop's clothes. But if Shore didn't have a witness it would be his word against Shore's. Shore could look like a vindictive, loose-mouthed liar. Why would a magistrate take the unsupported word of Shore against the word of a conscientious officer? No magistrate would do so. Then Jason remembered how the coroner's jury had listened to him, cleared him, and offered him an inevitable vindication of that sense of exultation he had felt standing in the rain, having just fired the gun. The vindication now seemed to belong with the big bang of the gun. It was a mysterious assurance that no one could ever take away from him, his big discovery of himself. Never again. That Shore, or a man like Shore, could dream of doing so was incredible. Jason went down into the garage and got in his car. When he came out into the sunlight again, he was burning with a sense of outrage.

The rest of the day and all night he nursed his sense of outrage. It was hard for him to make a plan to defend himself. But at 10:00 the next night he drove slowly down the street, looking for Al's address. The book, his excuse, was on the seat beside him. He was playing a dangerous game talking to a witness, and he knew it, but he trusted his ruthless decisiveness. Earlier that day he had refused to let his wife come home, and on this street tonight, with all his cunning, he planned to be the boss with Al Delaney.

It was a mild, clear night with music coming from open windows. No one was walking on the tree-lined street. Jason, trying to read the house numbers from the car, realized that he had gone up too far. Just as he turned, one hand on the wheel, ready to back up, a wild, piercing shriek shattered the silence. It rose in a long, unbroken, protesting, agonizing wail that echoed along the street and over the houses. Even Jason trembled. He had never heard such a wail. He thought a woman was being murdered or raped. He waited in the silence that followed. Automatically he had opened the car door so he could jump out and investigate. Now he closed the door slowly and carefully. Jason was not in uniform nor on duty. If a police car came along, his colleagues would ask what he was doing here. Up the street, a dog released as his master opened the door, barked frantically, then came loping down the street past Jason's car and across the road to the big, dark house opposite the Al Delaney address. In this house there was only one upstairs light. Circling around, the dog suddenly yapped frantically at a figure, a young man coming out of the dark alley who fled over lawns down to the next corner, the barking dog racing after him. Still Jason didn't move. He was minding his own business.

Up and down the street, as doors and windows opened, neighbors came out, calling to each other, and one by one they headed down the street past Jason's car. A stout man in his shirtsleeves, J. C. Rollins, the tailor and the dog's owner, hurried up the street, a leash in his hand, calling, "Hector, Hector, shut up, Hector. Here, Hector." Some 20 of the neighbors were now gathered in front of the big house that still had only one lighted upstairs window. Old Mrs. Frisbee—of the Frisbee jewelry family, once the owner of five stores. She now rented three apartments in her house, living on the top floor with her subdued alcoholic son—came out in a beautiful, flowered, velvet dressing gown. Her son, in his shirtsleeves, drowsy, half asleep, and startled, trailed her. And young Mrs. Ryerson, as thin as a rail and always so neat, though she had had five children, one of them retarded, appeared on the street. Dr. Atlee and his wife joined her. Dr. Atlee, the geophysicist, never seen by his neighbors, was actually there on the street with his wife when her two young friends, the neglected wives, came down the street, shyly approaching her. He was lean, young, and close-cropped. These neighbors, gathering on the sidewalk in front of the dark house, who hardly spoke to each other all year long, passing on the street, now all acted like old friends. Why in hell doesn't one of them go to that door instead of standing there gaping, Jason thought contemptuously. Then he saw a striking girl crossing the street, and he watched her alertly. She had come from Al's address. As she passed under the street light, it shone on her long, straight, black hair. She held herself apart, just listening. Jason wondered whether she might be Mrs. Delaney. The dog, still barking, returned to its owner, Mr. Rollins, who put it on its leash while talking to Dr. Atlee and pointing excitedly down the street at the corner house. Finally the two of them headed for the corner house and the alleyway where the fugitive and the pursuing dog had vanished. They walked with a resolute stride like men who understood they might find a woman in that house murdered or beaten. The neighbors watched. Jason also watched the men go to the door. In two minutes they returned, laughing. As yet no one had ventured into the unlighted house where neither door nor window had opened; it was now the most peaceful house on the street. Then, as Jason had expected, the police car came, and two officers, whom Jason couldn't recognize, got out, talked to the neighbors, stood looking at the house, then headed to the door, and knocked. They were admitted.

Jason felt trapped in the car. If he suddenly drove away his quick departure might be noticed and reported to the officers, so he could only slump back, waiting. Another car drove up. A middle-aged man, a doctor carrying his bag, hurried into the house, then everything slowed down. Finally the two policemen came out, and neighbors gathered around them. Jason couldn't hear a word. The policemen took their time, turning back to answer a question, then they sat in their car and talked for five minutes before they left.

Getting out of his car, Jason went over to the neighbors and mingled, listening and looking into faces that were full of friendly excitement. The fat man spoke to Jason as if they were old friends. Indeed, they were all old friends now. These neighbors, who had been apathetic to each other all year long, shared the excitement of being close to some terrible violence, and they found each other absorbing. They all had something to say. They listened to each other with respect. The fat man said to Jason, "Women are funny. They really are, you know. Imagine that dame in the corner house! I say to her, 'We thought you might be molested, assaulted,' She's in a dressing gown and she smiles a little and says, 'No such luck!' Imagine after that God-awful scream. No such luck! Good-looking too, about 40, I'd say." While he talked, he kept watching the darkened house, because the doctor was still in there. No one had known much about the mother and daughter who lived in the house. But now they all knew the girl's gentleman friend spent a lot of time there, and earlier that evening the girl had gone out, then returned home unexpectedly and found her young man in bed with the mother. She had rushed into the bathroom and cut her wrists, the cops had said. The awful scream had come from the mother who had followed her daughter to the bathroom. Their scared lover had run. The daughter hadn't done a very good job on her wrists.

Then Jason saw the girl he thought might be Mrs. Delaney, standing apart, still by herself. The charming man with the clipped hair, Atlee, and his wife, had crossed the road and gone in. The girl, reluctant to leave, stared at the one lighted window in the house of the girl with the slashed wrists. Her face in that street light, full of shock and restless excitement, had a kind of life in it that Jason had never known in a woman. Finally she too crossed the road to her own place. Jason waited a few minutes, watching her house. He went to the entrance and rang the upstairs bell. The girl came hurrying downstairs.

"Does Al Delaney live here?"

"Mr. Delaney isn't in."

"Are you Mrs. Delaney?"

"No. Can I help you?"

"When will he be in?"

"It's hard to say. What's it about?"

"I'm returning a book of his. I'm Jason Dunsford. A policeman."

"Oh! Didn't I see you across the street?"

"Probably. A little excitement, eh?"

"A policeman? Just standing there?"

"I'm off duty. I met Mr. Delaney when I stopped a car and later we had a talk and I liked talking to him. Since then something came up. Look, maybe I could talk to you."

"What's it about?"

"Well, it's confidential." He looked around. "If I could come in for a minute. . . ."

"I'm rather busy," she said. "Sorry." But her polite tone and smile was a condescension that stung him because she stepped out on the stoop, half closing the door behind her, making him feel she wouldn't have him in the house. "Now, officer, what's this about?" she asked curtly.

"Well, the man who wrote this book. . . ."

"Shore?"

"Yeah, Shore."

"I see," she said, appraising him. Then her manner changed.

"Well, come in," she said casually.

"Thank you," he said.

Following her up the stairs and then into the living room, he couldn't believe she belonged to a bearded guy like Al Delaney. She even looked out of place in her own living room. She had her own clean line and simple clothes. Under the overhead light he had noticed how severe was the part in her black hair; but the room was untidy. She had to take up a lovely Chinese dressing gown so that he could sit down.

"Now," she said and paused with her back to him, neatly folding the gown, "do you collect books, officer?"

"Collect," he said, surprised. "Why, no," and he was angry at how boyish the tone of his answer had been.

"Oh well, you see, I once knew a policeman who collected stamps. Anyway, Mr. Delaney certainly liked to talk to people about these books. It's too bad he's not here."

"It's too bad, yes," he said. "We kidded around about Shore. Do you know Shore?"

"Yes, I know Shore."

"Do you like him?"

"Not much."

"Good for you," he said with satisfaction as he leaned forward. "I gave him a ticket." He tried to smile. "Not a punch on the nose. Just a ticket." She smiled. The interest in her eyes encouraged him. "Yeah, you see, Shore thought he sized me up. Lots of people think they size up an officer."

"I see," she said, "Look, why don't I get you a drink?" On her way to the kitchen she called out, "Well, I wouldn't presume to size you up, but that was quite a picture of you in the papers. You looked like a general who had just accepted the surrender of all the Indian nations." She returned with a bottle of Scotch, some water, and two glasses. He searched her face for that exciting expression he had seen out on the street while she had stared at the house where the girl had slashed her wrists; now it wasn't the same face. She was too cool, too expensive, too aloof, and she made him feel like an employee.

Pouring him a stiff drink and taking a smaller one herself, she said, "I've seen two pictures of you now, haven't I?"

"I guess you have."

"You take a good picture."

"The first one was a kind of portrait taken quite a while ago."

"That last one—you and the coroner—that was a very striking picture."

"I'm glad you liked it."

187

Jason emptied his glass, and his eyes shifted from her legs to her face. He wanted to concentrate on her lovely legs, yet he kept returning to her face. He didn't know what he expected, but he knew he expected something. He lifted his glass again, and holding her eyes, he didn't notice the glass was empty. Only a drop touched his lip.

"I don't understand why you're so concerned about Eugene Shore," she said with a shrug. "He's just a writer."

"A big one, so they say."

"Who says?"

"Your Mr. Delaney for one."

"Well, after all, he's been a kind of special fan. But you," she said, leaning forward, "I'm sure Shore is not the rage of the cop world."

"You know," he said, seeking a moment of dignity, "we don't especially like being called cops." Before she could speak, he went on, "Anyway, a man like Shore can make a lot of trouble. Mr. Delaney is his good friend, and a nice easy guy himself, I'm sure. Why we should want to hurt each other, I don't know." The whiskey warmed him, he was pulled toward her by the grudging curiosity in her face. Suddenly he wanted very much to satisfy her, and he began telling her all kinds of little things about himself, about talking to Al, how he had given the Shore book to his wife, and how he had seen, after reading Shore himself, that his devotion to his wife and his tolerance had been no more than a sentimental, useless feeling. He was sure his openness was impressing her, and his knowingness about himself, too, and he said: "Why should a man like Shore want to meddle in my life? I have the feeling it shouldn't be allowed to happen."

"Shouldn't be allowed?" and she raised her eyebrows.

"It's not right."

"Right?" She smiled indulgently. "Well, I see I certainly didn't size you up. You don't sound like that big man in the picture."

"No, well—that's just a picture."

188

"So I see." Her contempt was so poorly concealed that he grew confused. He poured himself another drink. She slumped back on the sofa into a sensual slouch. He reached for what he was sure they shared, no matter what her tone, saying, "You don't like this man either, do you?"

"Shore is just a meddler," she said with a careless wave of her hand. "But I suppose in your position you have to think he's an important man. I don't blame you."

"You wouldn't mind if Mr. Delaney didn't show up as Shore's witness, would you?"

"Frankly, the sight of Shore standing alone would amuse me. Yes."

"If you talked to Mr. Delaney. . . ."

"Now really, I don't know that I want to understand you." But she came leaning forward a little. "Just what do you mean?" Then he knew she was listening. His wife, who loved him, had never been willing to listen carefully, even in their best moments, when he talked about another man. He realized that his brow was wet. He was sweating. Why was this girl who had shown contempt for him willing to listen now? Suddenly she smiled. It was a slow, encouraging, appreciative smile that warmed and lifted him. He thought she saw something in him she had missed, and again he felt that exalted sense of himself as a man who knew that when things got out of order good people wanted them put right. He believed she felt this power in him now; it made her want something from him. What was she waiting for him to say? In this silence that had the same expectancy that had followed the wild scream out on the street, his eyes went to a run on her stocking. It hadn't been in the stocking when she first sat down. It curved around her calf. She said idly. "Shore drinks, you know. He's often on the street quite drunk."

"Well?"

"Well, what happens if you pick up a drunk?"

"It's eight hours in the tank."

"Well," she said with finality.

"Well, what?" She only smiled. Then he looked at her thoughtfully and said: "You'd really like that guy to look bad, wouldn't you? You're alright."

"All right. . . ."

"Never mind. What street?"

"Oh!" And then for the first time she laughed. "There's that bridge over the ravine, not the old one, and above the bridge an intersection where the streets all come together like spokes in a wheel. Well, he lurches across there every Thursday late at night, or so he says, anyway. It's Shore's story, not mine." Looking at her watch, she stood up. "I've got friends coming in about now. Well, good luck."

"It's here," he said boldly.

"What's here?"

"The luck."

"What?"

"Here with you," he said, and as she moved with him toward the door, he slipped his arm around her.

"Oh, don't be silly," she said curtly. He felt the cut from the curt tone all the way downstairs and out onto the street. Yet somehow he knew her disdain didn't matter.

Seven days later, sometime after midnight, Eugene Shore was struck by a hit-and-run driver. He died on the way to the hospital. There was the smell of liquor on him.

24

Naturally Lisa trembled when her boss handed her the newspaper at lunchtime. Her boss, a sandy-haired, short man who thought he was homely, had always liked Lisa because she made him feel he could be attractive to a woman. "Al and you were friends of Shore's, weren't you?" he asked. "It's a good picture, isn't it?" he said while she stared at the front-page picture. It was the one with Mr. Shore wearing the beaver hat.

"Good God," she whispered. "What'll this do to Al?" and thought she was going to cry and fled, clutching the newspaper.

Her boss called after her sympathetically: "Lisa, maybe you want to take the afternoon off. Maybe you want to talk to Al."

She could hardly drive home with her foot trembling on the gas pedal and her stomach in a nervous knot. As soon as she got in, she took a hot bath. She took the telephone off the hook, swallowed two tranquilizers, and went to bed. It was after six when she woke.

She put the telephone back on the hook, made a pot of coffee, and then, sitting in the kitchen, tried to read the newspaper stories about Shore while she listened and waited. She couldn't concentrate. She burst into tears. She had to get up and wander around the house. Tears running down her cheeks, her arms folded around herself in a hug, she noticed that the house needed cleaning. It had been untidy ever since Al had left. Every time she thought of Shore, more tears came with twisted emotion, as if she were a spectator. She told herself Shore was a good, rare man and felt great sad pity for him. She kept going from the front window to the back of the house, holding her head in both hands. While listening apprehensively, a picture of Jason Dunsford's face popped horribly into her mind. That picture, the one standing with the coroner, the one with the big, bullying, disdainful, exultant grin that widened in appreciation as her despair deepened. She seemed to have only a little time before a terrible cry for absolution came from the depths of her natural human warmth, before something struggling within her took control of her mind and her heart and filled her with remorse. Yet she didn't know what this something was or why it scared her and made her desolate. It was like something she had been told about a long time ago, and hadn't believed in, because she couldn't feel it; she had never really believed there was anything outside herself to quarrel with, fear, or seek answers from, or console her in lonely nights, or whisper to her when she took a wrong step in the day. Now something there to be dreaded, was slowly bringing her closer to collapse, and yet she followed the street sounds attentively. The telephone rang.

"Oh, Al," she said in relief. "Thank God you called," as if she knew now that her real absolution could come only from Al. "I can't know how you feel about Shore," she blurted out. "He was part of your life. Oh, Al."

"I know," he said, "I feel cut off. I feel lousy." They exchanged protests against the luck of it, and wondering regrets and upsetting silences.

"Well, the paper says the funeral's to be private," she said.

"It's alright. I've talked to Mrs. Shore."

"She knows about you?"

"Shore had written to her just a week ago. She's back from New York. Starkey Kunitz came up with her. Imagine."

192

"I'll be there if you want me to, Al."

"I'll call for you."

"No. I'd rather just meet you there."

"Why?"

"I don't know."

"Lisa, I'm coming over—now."

"No."

"Why?"

"Last time it was too rough an experience. Now it wouldn't be any better. It would be worse," she insisted nervously. "I just don't want it."

"You heard my voice. You said, 'Thank God.'"

"I was upset. I was lonely."

"I'm coming over now."

"No. I'm getting myself together. Look, I'll be at the funeral."

"The funeral! That's not for three days. Why won't you see me?" he asked anxiously. "Why shouldn't you see me? What's the matter?" His urging began to shake her. "What is it?" he repeated. "No, tell me. What is it?"

She wanted to tell him about the cop, how afraid she was of the cop. And yet immediately, even in her anguish, it occurred to her that the last man on earth she had to be afraid of was that cop. She would be the last woman in the world he would want to hear from; it was just common sense. Al was the one she was afraid of. His voice, breaking her up, reminded her that she had never been able to hide anything from him. He had always been able to walk in on her and take her over, and he was doing it again. If he were there now, she would throw herself at his feet and say: "I was only thinking about you." Shuddering, she hung up on him quickly. The nerves in her legs were twitching. She began to massage them gently.

Finally she got up to get some coffee. Then, in a trance, she stared at the shiny, white, enamel surface of the kitchen table. There had been a tone in Al's voice, a different, strange tone. That tone suddenly became significant. Brooding over it, she grew fascinated. It struck her that Al had felt something in her, or about her, that he didn't recognize and that wherever he was now, he would be wondering about her. Maybe it would be better if he could go on wondering, maybe he should have to keep turning her over in his mind again and again. Slowly, she lifted the cup of coffee to her lips. Her hand was steady. She lit a cigarette and for the first time looked quietly thoughtful.

25

A new and attractive reticence of manner grew on her the next day. After work, when she came home and put her car in the garage and then came around to the front of the house, she met Mrs. Atlee, loaded with parcels.

"How are you, Mrs. Atlee?" she called.

"Oh, hello, Miss Tolen." Mrs. Atlee's face was suddenly unfamiliar. Some new interest was in it. Lisa couldn't imagine her own face telling Mrs. Atlee any secrets or that Mrs. Atlee's lively little face could ever have anything in it to alarm her. "You always look so fresh and collected," Mrs. Atlee said.

"I must say, you look rather sparkling, too."

"I'm in a good mood."

"I'm just myself."

"Everything looks good and feels good right now," Mrs. Atlee said.

"It must be the weather."

"No, my husband stayed home the last two nights like he's discovering me. It must be my left ear or big toe or something." The pretty little woman laughed and glowed.

"You'll never know—and maybe he won't either." Lisa said.

In the vestibule she listened for a sound upstairs. Then, climbing the stairs, she went right to the kitchen, opened the refrigerator, turned on the stove, and wished she could have a meal out with someone. Then she decided that scrambled eggs and toast would be enough for her. When she had eaten, she made a pot of tea. She poured herself a second cup, then didn't like to think of herself sitting in her kitchen drinking cup after cup of tea. Instead, she thought she would wash her hair. She took off her dress and tossed it on the bed. In the bathroom with the taps running, filling the basin, she leaned to the mirror to study her face, then suddenly stiffened, her heart thumping, and quickly turned off the taps. With the water running, she hadn't heard the sound at the front door. She grabbed at her little flimsy negligee, and opened the door.

Al stood at the top of the stairs.

"Hello," he said. "What's the matter?"

"You startled me."

"Are you alright?"

"You shouldn't walk in on me."

"Well, I had to," he said. As he came toward her, looking untrimmed, rumpled, and tired, he suddenly smiled. Something in the smile, not his sudden appearance, humiliated her. This utterly unexpected humiliation was bewildering. "I was going to wash my hair," she said awkwardly, so she could turn her back on him, and added: "Just a minute. I'll put something on." But he followed her into the bedroom and sat down on the end of the bed. Then he leaned back on his elbow and on the dress she had tossed on the bed.

"You're sitting on my dress," she said.

"Oh, sorry." He handed her the dress which she held in both hands as she sat down in the chair by the dressing table, and when he, in turn, went back to his position on the bed, they were making almost the same picture they had made many months ago after she had met him and had brought him home, and then, in the morning, there in the all white bedroom he had wakened and watched her sitting in this chair by the dresser, and she had on this same frilly little negligee.

196

"Lisa, look," he said, feeling her pulling away from him, "I know I walked out of here."

"Yes. Where did you go?"

"Mrs. Burnside's. She gave me a little room."

"Right back where you started from, and some dear little college girl—"

"Cut it out, Lisa."

"A girl who couldn't help liking you. You could make her laugh."

"Oh nuts."

"Did you make her laugh all the way to the bed?"

"Cut it out. Look, Shore's dead."

"I know he's dead."

"I've got to talk about him." Then he turned away, sighing. "It's all been a mighty strange business."

"Sudden death is always strange."

"Not just the death. The whole night."

"I went to bed early."

"I didn't." Swinging his legs over the end of the bed, he sat up, but his eyes remained on the floor. His face, showing his feelings, upset her because she knew the changing emotions in it involved her as much as Shore, and he was all wound up. "Yes, a crazy night for me," he said. "All Shore. I was in the room working. It was late. I had been going good. But something had come up, a flaw, in my view. I saw it after talking to him. You see, Lisa," he said, bringing her in spite of herself, under the spell of his warmth, "pushed to its logical conclusion Shore's world is a world of complete anarchy. Literature—anarchism's last hurrah! We knew about that. Yet it isn't true of Shore. There's the whole damned mystery. For some mysterious reason, it's something more than anarchy. I think I know why. I think it's some kind of warmth or love he has for all his characters, big or small, a love and respect for the mystery of the dignity of their personalities. But there was this Goddamned flaw. I was sitting in the room feeling pretty cynical. The room was at the back of the house. It was late, and I had just got up and stood at the window, looking out over alleys

197

and chimneys, the radio turned down, the way I like it, then the news came on, and I heard about Shore. When did you hear about it, Lisa?"

"Next morning in the paper."

"Yeah," he said. He remained lost in his thoughts a moment, then went on. "There I was imagining I was talking to the guy, and right then he was dead. Just when I needed a little more. Just a little more and I could see the whole thing. But just the same, aside from the work, Lisa, I felt such a hurt, such a strange wrench in me. Look. He's been a part of you and me. . . ." The truth was in his voice, and as he kept on, he began to soothe away her fear of listening to him. He had always been able to make her feel she was the only one who could understand the emotional impulse behind his talk. After making love, while they were resting, he could talk to her, and because of the emotional energy in him, even when the words came slowly, have her feel he was still making love. He was lulling her now, his voice caressing and lifting her up.

"I couldn't stay in the room," he said. "I had to get out. Other nights, walking, thinking of the work, I seemed to get deep into Shore's world. I could fill the streets with his characters. Now the streets were just empty caverns, I felt lonely, and had to get in somewhere, and I went into an all-night restaurant just two blocks away from the room, a place where I used to have coffee after a night with the taxi. I sat at the counter, beside two girls. They had good figures and pretty, easy faces. They were with two heavy, older men who just listened, bored and uncomfortable. The guys had nothing to say even to each other. The girls evidently worked in the shoe department of a big department store. They were exchanging insights on what you could learn of a woman's life from her choice of shoes and the way she treated her feet. A woman's life showed in her feet, they agreed. Women who had no respect for their feet, had no respect for themselves! "What do you say about a woman who jams her toes into a shoe and gets them all twisted?" one asked. "I'd say she's always putting her foot in where it isn't wanted," and the other said, "A smart guy could know a lot about a woman as soon as he gets her to take off her shoes," "I know a girl who always keeps her shoes on when she makes love," the other one said. And in the mood I was in, with Shore laid out in an undertaker's parlor only a few blocks away, I reached for anything diverting, and I thought, Why not? The meaning of a woman's life—all in her feet. A good timely subject for a Ph.D. thesis to be laid on Dr. Morton Hyland's desk. The myth of the female foot. All of life told in a woman's foot. I was trying to snicker to myself; then I thought, wait a minute! It's true you can make anything you want to make out of a foot or a face or anything that gets into your imagination. If a thing is big enough and always changing, you look at it once, you make one thing out of it, another thing at another time, eh? It's life, isn't it? Life is big enough and mysterious enough and bewildering enough and there are no final answers about it. None at all. Only questions. So you can make absolutely anything you want to make out of life. You'll be hit on the head, of course, by the authorities, who have agreed to make their own thing out of it. But what the hell. You know they themselves are only making what they need to make to keep their authority. Now look, Lisa, maybe this is just a little thing, but look—my surprise stirred my whole being as I thought. It's the same with Shore. It's the same with Lisa. I make what I want to make out of them. Lisa, Lisa." He smiled. "You don't exactly look as if you understood the lift this gave me."

"No, I don't."

"Oh, come on, Lisa."

"Damn it all," she said, finding relief in sudden anger. "I'm not a body of work you can put away for a while, then come back to and look at. That's alright for Shore, and maybe it's the way you should have felt about his work all along, but I'm alive. You said to me, 'What are you, anyway?' As if I could ever tell you! As if anyone could ever tell you! And if they could, I'd be dead. And you don't seem to understand that what you make of me may have nothing to do with what I am. I don't know whether you'd have the courage to take me just as I am—"

She faltered, outraged because he listened with such complete approval; then changing, she seemed to know secretly that nothing more should be said.

"Just the same," he said standing up slowly, "To get it all straight, and in fairness to Shore. . . ."

"About what?"

"That cop."

"Who cares now about that cop?"

"This is about Shore, Lisa. That cop—"

"To hell with him now, Al," then controlling her nervousness she added gently, "We just can't believe Shore's dead, can we?"

"I know he's dead. I know—" His voice broke and he tried to smile. "The trouble is, every little thing he ever said to me comes so close now it hurts. Everything hurts. Things seem so real, so painfully real. Not just the cop. Things I wanted to say myself. I've been up all night on this. I can't stop thinking. Listen, Lisa." Then she realized that he was talking to her as if he were in bed beside her, the only one he could talk to and she was afraid to speak. She felt shame. But while he talked, she had to hide her growing wonder, for she could see how the emotional shock of Shore's death had made Al feel that his perceptions, coming at this time, were true because he was so moved.

"The other day at that inquest I took a dirty crack at Shore," Al said. "I said to him: 'What do you think you are? Your own church?' Lisa, I didn't know how right I was." His voice breaking, he went on: "Oh, it's a lovely idea, Lisa. His temperament! His church!" She could only nod, though her mouth trembled, half in anguish. When his face lit up and he stood up excitedly and came and sat on the end of the bed, she saw that he thought he had found the one right pattern for his work. Then she closed her eyes so he couldn't look into them and see that her sudden wild surprise had lifted her fiercely. She could believe that he had this eagerness now because it was now, and Shore was gone. "Go on, Al, go on," she whispered desperately. "Yeah. Shore's temple—where his outlaws are all in his light, that baffling light, all free to become aware of

200

the adventurous possibilities of their mysterious personalities." He was too moved to go on for a moment. "Lisa . . . I feel I've been in that temple," he said, "I've felt the exciting warmth of these strange outlaws. It does something for me. Others bigger than I am in their humanity—their fates. I become a little bigger myself—yet without caring about it. See what I mean? Now I can make my own banquet hall, stand at the door and keep the riffraff out. Crimes and punishments? Ah, no. No pious penitents sneak by the door. Dostoevski? Hell, No! His Raskalnikof! Let him pound on the door and tear his hair shirt. What a little man! A scholar, I suppose, like me, I suppose, stirred up by some kind of an existential thrust to be above the bookkeeping phony society he lived in, well, what did he do? Did he have any respect for the longing in him? He turns thug. Knocks off some poor little woman. There's a big league protest for you! Then Dostoevski takes about 600 pages to get the guy trapped so he can repent and be in the wringer for about ten years and become very humble and respectable, so he can fit into the society he despised. Brought to heel! Well, in my banquet hall, Lisa, no one gets in who has been brought to heel, and. . . ."

"What are you saying?" Lisa asked. Pale, and staring at him wide-eyed, she half believed that the things he said were his way of telling her that he could know about the cop, because he knew her and she was a little frightened, remembering how he had always searched her face. Yet it seemed to her that in his telling, he had been trying to comfort her and buoy her up. But how could he possibly know about the cop? "What are you trying to tell me?" she stammered.

"Yes, I guess I'm a little excited," he said.

"You made it sound like a poem," she said. "Maybe it's all just a poem. Maybe that's all you really want it to be, all it needs to be."

"No, I mean it," he said, coming over to her.

Slumping back, looking up at him expectantly, she felt tempted to take the risk and tell him, and she trembled, feeling all the thrill of the risk.

"This has all been a nightmare," he said gently. "I've made

you suffer through it. Sometimes I've felt like a monster. Such a monster! I often couldn't believe I'd ever be here with you, feeling such joy, such lightness about my work."

"Dear God, no," she whispered, standing up.

Her negligee slipped from her shoulder, baring one breast, but her black hair swung over the nipple. "No," she protested fiercely, "I shouldn't be here now." Then, suddenly stricken, she realized that as soon as she had seen him coming along the hall, smiling, she must have known she had betrayed his independence, his defiance, his pursuit of his own vision, with her tragic meddling. She started to cry.

"Lisa, what did I say?"

"I can't leave anything alone. I can't. I really can't, you know. I'm the monster," she sobbed. But as he gathered her negligee about her, fumbling at the left shoulder, his gentle, unknowing concern for her only deepened her torment. Raging at herself and at him, too, she did what she had done in Rome, confronting him outside St. Peter's: pulling fiercely away, she withdrew into a darkness so deep in her that he couldn't follow. He could only wait, stirred and expectant. The last of the daylight from the window had gone. Shadows fell across the room. Then, in her deepening withdrawal, she felt a chill in her whole being, as if this darkness she sought and found now was a kind of death touching her; she shivered; then in a panic, despairing, she was sure that when she had been sitting with the cop in her apartment, so cool and apart from him, she had been drawing on this same chilling darkness. "It's in everybody," she whispered. "It must be."

"What?" he asked, bewildered.

In the shadows, she couldn't see his eyes and stepped closer to him. But when her head went back and her hair swung back and she was ready to unburden herself defiantly, she looked so much like herself as he knew her that he smiled, his alarm vanishing and while he smiled, there came to her a little reassuring whisper. "No, look at him. Doesn't he look just right?"

He had come closer to the window. His bearded face was

on the last beam of light and he looked so full of certitude about himself and her that she stared at him, full of wonder. He looked as he had looked in Rome, when full of restless energy, imagination and challenge, he tried to hurl himself into the wild lives of those antique figures on their pedestals. It was the way she wanted him to be. In a wild surge of love she told herself that she might have long nights of torment and doubts about herself and regrets and even some tears. Yet they wouldn't matter, even if it went on the rest of her life, she could endure and live with torment, even make something out of it good for both of them. "Al," she whispered, "It's just that I don't know what to make of it."

"Ah, I know," he said, taking her in his arms. When he touched her, and as soon as she felt his lips brushing her neck and shoulders, she began to shake with relief. Her eyes filled with tears. Hugging her again, he laughed a little and while he held her, made her desperate for more of this relief, and she pulled away, let the negligee fall to the floor, hurrying, then she stretched out naked on the bed. Her hair was spread out on the pillow, her eyes were closed; one arm was behind her head, and she waited for him. On the end table by the bed was an electric clock. She heard the soft whirring, and hated it, for now there should be no movement of time. Then he came kneeling on the bed, silent, looking down at her. Hurrying for relief for her whole being, she reached for him, and for the first time in their lovemaking, she put him in her.

26

It got dark in the room, but she did not turn on the bed light. Her head lay on his shoulder. They rested and smoked, talking easily. He had been in touch with the publisher, he said, and had promised to deliver the manuscript in a month. There would be no problem. The publisher had picked up an enthusiastic interest. "You know something, Lisa," he said quietly, "I honestly believe I understand Shore's work now better than he understood it himself."

"Do you think Shore would agree?"

"Well," and he paused. "Oh, of course not." and they both laughed.

"Don't you find it getting a little chilly in here?" she asked. "I think I'll put something on. How would you like a drink?"

"No drink. I've got to work. I'd fall asleep."

"How do you do it . . . without sleep."

"Do what?"

"Cut it out," she said, giggling. "How about a cup of coffee."

"No, tea."

"That's a funny thing."

"What?"

"I've started drinking tea, too."

While Al was dressing, she made a pot of tea. Then they sat in the kitchen and he smoked three of her cigarettes. He might as well take the package, she said. No, she had a carton in her bureau drawer. "Wait, I'll get you one," she said, because he was going back to his room to work. He asked her if he should call for her in the morning so they could go to the funeral together. Again she told him it would be easier to meet him there. "Wait a minute, Al," she said when he was leaving. "My key."

"Your key?"

"You have my key."

"I thought it was my key."

"Leave it here, Al."

"What is this, Lisa?"

"I don't like to think anyone can walk in on me."

"Anyone?"

"No one is ever going to walk in on me," she said calmly. "Never again."

"I don't know just what that means."

"I shouldn't be an open house for someone to come in and poke around in," she said shrugging. "Now come on, Al, you know a caller should have to knock."

"I see," he said, regarding her steadily. "Well, fair enough," and he handed her the key solemnly. "I'll see you," he said. She kissed him and he went. Then she sat down at the end of the kitchen table and was very still, reflecting. Finally she got up, hurried into the bathroom, and took a cold shower. The sting of the cold water made her jump around slapping at her flesh, and when she got out of the shower she felt fresh, exhilarated, and restless. She couldn't stay in the house. She got dressed and went out. Loafing along, she began to marvel at Al's sureness now about himself and his work. The rhythm of her walking began to stimulate her imagination. If everything could be working out for Al, she thought, and if he was full of his own importance, surely it could be taken as a sign of new good things impending. Some people not of her frame of mind would wonder if there could be a natural pattern to the events shaping around her. She dwelt on this with some fascination. There could be a perfection in the form of these happenings, they would say, a form being shaped without any visible mark of a director's hand, a kind of terrible beauty in a pattern around Shore's death, and she had just a little right place in it; a pattern so inevitable that it would have the approval of nature itself.

She had slowed down to look around and see where she was, thinking she would get the *New York Review of Books, Paris Match,* and the *New Statesman* to see what was going on outside. But on Yonge, passing Isaacs' art gallery, she stopped, turned back, and looked at the big painting displayed in the window. It was awful. It fell to pieces. Isaacs, that busy man, had such a strange, trendy taste. Yet she felt drawn in to the gallery. Not for a year had she been in an art gallery. The girl at the desk took off her glasses.

"Why, hello there, Miss Tolen. Where have you been all this time?" In Isaacs' they knew everybody. Six other patrons were in the gallery. Elegantly alone, she sauntered from picture to picture, apparently self-contained. A painting by a man she had never heard of caught her eye and she looked, walked away, came back, sat down in front of this painting, lit a cigarette, wondering what was happening on the canvas that had caught her attention. Soon she grew absorbed in discovering secret tensions in the picture held together in a mystery of form that gave her a wondering satisfaction. She remained there lost in thought, the last one to leave the gallery.

When she got home she put on a house dress, wrapped a big handkerchief around her head, and began to clean up her house with furious energy. It took her two hours. The kitchen was cleaner than it had been all year long. Every stick of furniture in the house was dusted, shiny, and in place. Then she took a bath. Soon she was sound asleep. In the morning when she went downstairs to the door to get the newspaper, the morning sunlight, drenching the street, came reaching for her so warmly it took her breath away. Over her coffee she read about Eugene Shore and again felt carried along in a pattern that had its strange rightness. There were columns about Shore, wonderful, glowing pieces. 'A unique artist who belonged to the world, yet was of this town.' Imagine. Probably the most remarkable artist the town had ever produced. He would become a classic. Already the academics were being quoted. There was a picture of the Shores' house, too. They were all too generous now. There were many quotes from the original Kunitz article on Shore's work; no scolding of Kunitz now. The newspapers must have been tipped off that he was coming to town.

27

Lisa decided to wear her black dress. It had such a simple, elegant expensive look to it. Her only piece of jewelry was that Syrian necklace her father had given her. Until now she had been avoiding her mirror. Her unsettled nerves and her lack of sleep had made her look wan. Now, facing the mirror, she hardly knew herself. She had an aloof, melancholy beauty—a woman with a secret, tragic awareness of the inevitability of things. She drove her car to the little church in grounds set far back from the street with the cemetery and all its old headstones behind it, sloping down to the ravine. Two bluebirds darted from the tall tree on the edge of the hill. You could almost see the Shore house from there, but not quite, for the new high-rise apartments blocked the view.

She was a few minutes late. There was Al all by himself, standing near the church door in his only dark suit, watching her come up the path. He had his funny, little, protective smile. "Oh, Al," she said, her hand going out to him.

"Come on, Lisa," he said gently. "We may not get a seat."

For a small, private service there were at least 200 people. No one paid any attention to Mrs. Shore's request for privacy. While an usher was leading Al and Lisa to a pew at the front,

Lisa could feel eyes turning on her, eyes in familiar, important faces. The president of the university, Dr. Stacey, with his inscrutable smile and good looks, was there, although he had never spoken a word to Shore. And there were men and women from the English department, editors and many middle-aged men and their wives from Shore's schooldays, who looked as if they had done very well. Lisa could only see the back of Mrs. Shore's head. The hair was gray, and her head remained bowed. This one head, never turning, made Lisa want to weep. The poor woman—the poor, dear woman—she thought.

The service was brief, but the sermon was too long. The young clergyman, impressed by his audience and the publicity, wanted to talk about the greatness of Shore's work but obviously hadn't had time to read a book. He quoted from Kunitz. At the end, when the mourners streamed out, Lisa and Al stood to one side of the entrance. "Kunitz asked me to have a drink with him," Al said.

The crowd of mourners breaking up in groups on the green lawn in front of the church waited, watching the entrance. Newspaper photographers had their cameras ready. A television camera set up on a tripod, looked 40 years out of date. Finally Mrs. Shore came out with Starkey Kunitz. The small, quietly elegant, sweet-faced woman attempted an appreciative smile for her friends, but her lips trembled. She stiffened, then recovering her serene, attractive dignity, she came down the steps with Kunitz who wasn't much taller than she was. His well-cut, dark-brown suit was rumpled, and his tie was a little off center from the collar of his white shirt. Yet it was as if he wouldn't have had it any other way. Portly, red-faced, nearly bald, with compelling, light-blue eyes, he had an air of splendid indifference. The newspapermen approached him diffidently, for in the way he held his head and in his level glance, he suggested very intimidatingly that he knew everything that could be known or was worth knowing, and now that he was in town he didn't have to look at the natives with any new curiosity: he had already looked at them and judged them. This was probably Starkey Kunitz' weakness; he had consulted his sources, got opinions from friends he trusted, read Eugene Shore, made his judgment, and now had no interest in taking a fresh look at the townfolk. What he had said remained engraved on tablets in the permanent body of the Kunitz work.

That beery old columnist, J. C. Hilton, with the long, reddish, drooping moustache, who was even portlier than Kunitz, even more like a real old British colonel, approached Kunitz. "Could I have a word now?"

"Forget about me," Kunitz said flatly. "This is not my funeral."

"A word about Eugene Shore—now that he's dead."

"Are you sure he's dead?" Kunitz asked blandly. "Weren't you all sure you had killed him off around here sometime ago? That's all now, please."

"Dr. Kunitz, I'm J. C. Hilton. I'm speaking for my publisher." No one on earth had ever called Kunitz "doctor." Yet, if you had done research, he could be called "doctor," especially if you approached him with Hilton's distinguished air! Kunitz did have a Ph.D. "The publisher would like to do a long piece, a full page exhaustive interview with you. And, sir—"

Looking down his nose, Kunitz said: "I don't know your publisher. I'm up here to pay my respects to Eugene Shore. Interviews? Tell him when I'm interviewed, I interview myself."

"The publisher would like us to have lunch with him. He'd like to honor you with either a lunch or a dinner. And we would like Dr. Morton Hyland to come. It would be his pleasure. For us, a real treat. It's time you two met."

"Thank you," Kunitz said. Reflecting, he added with a short laugh, "Dr. Hyland, eh? There's a beauty for you! I think he's crazy."

"Excuse me," Hilton said stiffly. "Excuse me," and he hurried away.

"I shouldn't be here, Al. I'll leave you now," Lisa said, touching his arm.

"Don't you want to meet Mrs. Shore, Lisa?"

"I couldn't bear to. Oh, no. I'd be in the way," she said

hastily, confusing him because he had never heard her say she'd be in the way. "I mean, you'll be talking to Kunitz, Al. I shouldn't be around."

"I've already talked to him."

"What did he say?"

"I gave him my own view of Shore."

"So?"

"He gave me a surprised funny look, and said, 'Go to it. Now we can afford to be tender.'"

"Well—"

"I told him I can't stop writing," he said and then looked around. "I feel a little like a vulture, Lisa. I wanted to say to Kunitz: 'We're vultures, you know.' But what disciple, what apostle, what critic, ever felt like a vulture? Dear God, there must be much more to it than picking Shore's bones, then putting him in the crypt of literature. In me now there's so much more. Why do I feel all this life, all this energy? Is it outrageous that I now feel so eager to work and so sure I have him in hand? I don't know, Lisa."

"Of course not. It's wonderful for you."

"I know. Look, Lisa, when will I see you?"

"Give me a few more days, Al. Give me a chance to feel right."

"I wonder," he said, looking at her. "We part, Lisa. Parting to meet again, meeting to look again," as if now, looking, he saw new aspects, missed shadows and silences and something else hidden in her that already quickened him. "What is it, Lisa?" he asked. "There's something—"

"You seem a little different, too, Al."

"There's nothing new, nothing mysterious, about me, Lisa."

"How do you know?"

"I'm going to start courting you, Lisa. I'll knock."

"I just might be at home," she said. "Bye-bye."

"So long," he said.

While she walked down the path in the shadow from the church, she knew he was following her with his eyes. Then suddenly she was all in sunlight. The intensely blue sky over-head, the brilliant sunshine, the lush green of the full blooming trees, the extravagantly gay yellow daffodils, and the bed of red tulips blooming like mad all opened up to her so warmly that she shivered as if in an embrace, as if she were being offered the approval of all ruthless, ripening nature for letting her love have its own law. It had all been said to her anyway; it had all come together in Al's wondering, reaching, approving smile.